CASTLE OF BONES

A Medieval Gothic Novella

By Kathryn Le Veque

KATHRYN LE VEQUE

NOVELS

ARE YOU SIGNED UP FOR KATHRYN'S BLOG?

You'll get the latest news and information on exclusive giveaways, exclusive excerpts, coming releases, sales, free books, cover reveals, and more.

Kathryn's blog followers get it all first. No spam, no junk.

Get the latest info from the reigning Queen of English Medieval Romance!

Sign Up Here

kathrynleveque.com

AUTHOR'S NOTE

Usually, when I write these spooky-themed novellas, they always revolve around a poem by Edgar Allan Poe. That's kind of been my "thing," and over the years, I've had a lot of fun interpreting Poe's work into a story. But this spooky tale is different—no inspiration from Poe, although it really feels like it.

This tale, in fact, is something I started many years ago but I wasn't sure where it was going, so I put it aside and went on to other things. But I very much wanted to finish it, someday, and was happy I had the time to finally do it and release it close to Halloween. I do love spooky, Gothic tales, and what's spookier than a castle made of bones?

I love to write about secondary characters in novellas like this, characters where I know I'll never live long enough to write them a full-length tale. In this case, we have Hermes de Norville, son of Hector de Norville and Evelyn de Wolfe.

Hermes and his older brother, Atreus, are some of my favorite secondary characters to write about during the original de Wolfe series and the de Wolfe Pack Generations. Two brothers, very close in age, with their grandfather Paris' hot head. They fight. They fight in front of their parents, in front of visitors, in front of siblings—those two are always throwing punches, and I find that hilarious.

However, since they're fairly minor secondary characters, I knew I'd never write them a full-length tale, so in 2021, I wrote a Halloween-inspired novella in which Atreus was the hero (Nevermore), and in this novella, we have his brother as the hero.

Hermes has thankfully grown up, but he's had some bad luck in his life. He's grown into a rather bitter man. I loved taking him from the journey of a scrapper of an adolescent to an accomplished, educated man with some baggage. But he's a de Norville and a de Wolfe, so honor is inherent in him. When he wants to do something good, he'll accomplish it or die trying.

Enter our heroine, Catrine.

If you've ever seen the movie *Dragonwyck*, with Vincent Price, the title character of Nicholas Van Ryn has a daughter named Catrine. Sad little girl. The actress who played her was adorable. Her name, and character, is the inspiration for my Catrine. And, much like *Dragonwyck*, the house (or castle, in this case) that the story revolves around is a house of many mysteries. But unlike Dragonwyck, our characters have a happy ending.

The usual pronunciation guide:

De la Pare—day-luh-pair-RAY

Gisla—GEES-luh

Without further ado, welcome to the Castle of Bones!

Hugs,

A castle layered with secrets…
A family living a curse…

Will a knight in shining armor be enough to save them?

Castle Draygon is a castle with more than one mystery. When Hermes de Norville rides into the village at the base of the castle, little does he know how his life is going to change. A chance meeting with a woman the villagers call the Angel of Death changes his stars, but an accident introduces him to a pair of women who will help him find his path to those stars.

And so begins a complex and dark tale.

Castle Draygon is rife with curses and legends, Hermes discovers. But above the whispers and rumors hovers an evil over the castle that controls its occupants. Hermes can't help his attraction to Catrine de la Pare, the woman known to the villagers as the Angel of Death, but Catrine's story is as complex as the legends behind Castle Draygon itself. Reeling from the loss of his wife and riddled with grief, Hermes finds direction when it comes to Catrine. She doesn't deserve the reputation she's been given by superstitious villagers, and it's up to Hermes to save Catrine and her brother, a man known as the Dragon, from the evil that hangs over Castle Draygon.

Can Hermes break the curse? Or will the evil in the tower overtake him, too?

Join Hermes and Catrine in a romantic Gothic Medieval tale.

PROLOGUE

Year of Our Lord 1295

"H ELP ME! OH, God, help me!"

A woman hung helplessly on a ledge, her bloodied fingers slipping away bit by bit as the waves far below her crashed against the rocks with violent intensity. He tried to reach her, but the winds were too strong, pushing against him. In desperation, he fell to his belly, hoping that it would be easier if he crawled. But the ground was soft, sucking at him, and making it almost impossible to gain headway.

He felt as if he was sinking.

"Hermes!" she screamed again. *"Help me!"*

There was such pain in her plea. It turned his stomach, forcing strength through his struggling limbs. He inched forward, wrestling against the violent storm that watered his eyes and deafened his ears.

"I'm coming!" he shouted in return. "Hold tight, do you hear? *Hold tight!"*

The woman gasped softly as her grip slipped again. "I cannot," she moaned. "If you do not hurry, all will be for naught!"

He knew that. God, he knew that. He forced himself to move, gaining leverage on the ground that was trying to swallow him. He had heard of quicksand but had never actually experienced it. He didn't know that any existed in England. Maybe all of it was concentrated on this one cliff, high above the furious sea. He wondered how he had gotten here. He couldn't even remember.

"Hermes!" The woman's voice was filled with panic now, no longer the simple terror she had earlier expressed. "Hurry, Hermes. *I'm slipping!*"

He struggled across the unstable ground. He was within a mere foot of her, but it might as well have been a mile. The wind was stronger now, the storm howling about his head. It was obvious that he was being prevented from reaching her in a timely manner. Either the storm wanted her to die, or they wanted him to fail. Or both.

One of her hands slipped off the ledge, and she screeched. In a burst of strength and anxiety, he propelled himself forward and managed to grab a couple of her fingers. But it was not enough. With the wind screaming and the storm lashing, her fingers slowly pulled from her grasp.

"No," she cried. *"No!"*

"I'm…trying," he grunted, and strained against the unimaginable forces opposing him. "Give me your other hand!"

She was beginning to hang limply now, her long hair tossed about by the powerful winds. Her fingers were itching from his hands as he squeezed, white-knuckled, trying to hold them tight.

"You promised," she said. "Why would you lie?"

He was desperate, angry now that she was accusing him of falsehood. He was endeavoring to save her, and she was turning on him.

"I have given you no falsehood," he growled, giving her a yank to try to shore up his grip. Instead, she slipped further, and he clamped down on her with his other hand, gaining a weak hold of her wrist. "You see? I've got you now. Give me your other hand and I'll pull you up."

She was sapped of her strength from the struggle to save her life. Her head lolled back as she dangled from the cliff, held in place only by his strong grip. She was like a body with no bones, spent and resigned, and when she looked up at him, her face was unclear and murky, like the churning depths of the sea. He couldn't even make out her eyes.

"Save me, Hermes," she murmured. "I need you."

He gazed at her, trying to make out her features and wondering, bleakly, why they all seemed to spill together like melting wax. He wasn't afraid, but she was puzzled. The wind seemed to die down as he continued to stare at her, his sky-blue eyes full of uncertainty.

"Who…?" he murmured. "Who *are* you?"

He thought she was gazing back at him, though he could not be sure. Her beautiful chestnut-colored hair whipped about wildly, striking them both. Then she brought her other hand up, the one he had begged so hard for, and she touched his fingers so tenderly that bolts of excitement shot through him until he could hardly breathe. Her eyes, for a brief moment, came into focus; they were an amazing shade of green, as dark leaves on a vine, but nearly translucent. Very clearly, he could see pieces of gold set deep in the field of green. They were mesmerizing.

"You don't know me," she whispered.

"If I knew you, I wouldn't have to ask your name," he replied. "Again, I ask who you are."

"One who needs you most of all."

"Does this One have a name?"

"One does."

"What is it?"

"When you find me, you'll know."

As he stared into her incredible eyes, her undefined, swirling mouth smiled. He thought it a beautiful smile. Suddenly, she came alive in his grip and braced her feet against the side of the cliff. Giving a violent pull, she wrenched herself from his grip.

"No!" he shouted.

Helplessly, she fell into the vortex of waves and rocks below. He reached out for her, clawing at the air in a vain attempt to save her. Quite clearly, he heard her voice before she hit the darkness and violence below, and the words sang to him like the voice of angels.

"*...you promised!*"

CHAPTER ONE

Year of Our Lord 1295
Somewhere in Northumberland

H E AWOKE WITH a start.

His heart was pounding in his ears and his body was covered with perspiration. The room was dark, and he blinked unsteadily, struggling to orient himself. Realizing that he was no longer on the cliff, no longer restrained by the sinking sand, and no longer a failure at saving a woman in distress, he let out a sigh and shakily scratched his head.

God, it was always the same damn dream.

For as long as he could recall, he had been having this nightmare, and it always ended the same. He woke up feeling as if he had just lost a battle.

The chamber around him was dark save the embers in the hearth that were smoking heavily. The air of the room was filled with a thick, dirty smell. But the smoke wasn't the only stench he could identify; on the bed beside him, a body stirred, and he glanced over, remembering the whore he had taken into his bed the previous night after too much wine and too much depression. She stank like a privy. He hadn't noticed it last night in the midst of his lust; now, he was surprised he could smell anything at all over the rank scent of alcohol on his own breath. Ripping the covers off the woman, he exposed her naked flesh.

"Get out," he growled.

A dark, curly head lifted, and sleepy eyes gazed at him. "But it's not yet dawn," she protested softly. "Come back to bed, lover. I'll make the night pass more pleasantly."

She reached for him, but he rose, his powerful nude body exposed in the dim light. The whore rolled onto her stomach, her eyes licking him hungrily.

"Aye, my love," she purred. "A gift from the gods, your body is. I've never seen such powerful legs, nor so slender a waist, nor a chest that seems hewn from pure marble. You're as perfect as a Grecian statue."

He ignored her as he put on his hose. The whore groaned. "Nay, my beauteous lad. Why must you cover your magnificent manroot? Your potency has filled me like nothing else, and believe me when I say that I've sampled enough to know."

He pulled on a boot. "I told you to get out."

Her words of praise were going unheeded, and a seed of desperation sprouted in her breast. "You have nothing to fear from me, my powerful lord. Even if I were to bear your son from our night of passion, know that I would not demand marriage or…"

He looked her in the eye. "You'll not demand anything from me. I'll not ask you again to leave. The next time, I'll simply throw you out on your arse."

Her smile fled. "So, the mighty Sir Hermes makes threats," she said in a low voice. "Last night it was wine and song. This morn, it's venom and fangs."

He put on his other boot and gazed at her; he held no expression, but the malice in the sky-blue eyes was obvious. He meant every word he said. The whore climbed from the bed and went in search of her clothing, her big bottom swinging saucily. Finding her own meager clothing, she bent over slowly, offering him a full view of the dark, overused thatch between her legs.

"I must say, I was not surprised by the power of your lovemaking," she said, her dark eyes glimmering. "Although you're not as tall as other knights I have known, you're several times more powerful. And your lower arms are the size of a mutton leg!"

Hermes cocked an eyebrow at her words, intended to be flattery. But they almost made him laugh. True, his lower arms were enormous, and so were his upper arms for that matter, but he'd never heard his limbs described as a piece of meat before. One woman had told him that the golden fuzz covering his arms reminded her of gold dust; another said it reminded her of the downy fluff on an infant's head.

As the whore chattered on about the size of his arms, Hermes actually found himself looking down at them, noting the blue veins that pulsed beneath the skin. He spread his hands open as if to examine them; he thought his hands rather small for the size of his arms, but they worked well enough. His wife had told him once that they were magical hands. He closed his hands and looked away. God, how he missed her.

"...and your shoulders are as broad as a full-grown tree. All of the power in your wide, wide shoulders make me giddy!"

The woman was prattling on and on. Hermes scratched his scalp, his golden-blond hair shorn close to his skull. He had the de Norville hair, fair and thick. When it grew long, it stuck straight up like straw, so he kept it cropped close for ease and comfort. He happened to glance at himself in the polished bronze mirror nailed to the wall of the chamber; a strong, stubbled jaw met his inspecting gaze. He was looking older than his thirty-something years; his eyes were circled from too much drink and not enough sleep. He rubbed his chin pensively. Living the lifestyle he had chosen over the past two years, he was amazed that he was still alive.

"…and your legs are as big around as posts. I have never seen so many muscles in a man's leg, and I've seen many a leg." The whore was pulling on her shoes, great brown leather things that were too big for her small foot. She was oblivious to the fact that he wasn't listening to her, or at least she pretended to be. "But your face, I must say, is the most handsome I've ever seen. Where do men come by such beauty?"

Hermes finished studying his face. He didn't see any beauty in it. He went in search of his tunic. "Close the door behind you."

He wasn't interested in her praise, that much was obvious. Dejected, the whore pulled her shawl about her shoulders, gazing at the blond, powerful man as he tossed his tunic over his magnificent torso. Her words to describe it had not been false; never had she seen finer. But now that the drink had worn off, he was cold and hard again, as he had been when he first entered the inn. But for those few hours while the ale settled deep in his veins, she had come to discover a few things about Sir Hermes de Norville, son of the House of de Norville.

He was a bitter, damaged man.

"Do you return to London now to see your children?" she asked, making one last attempt at pleasant conversation, hoping to stay in his good graces. "It's been a long time since I've been to London. Mayhap I could…"

He pulled a great leather surcoat over his tunic in preparation for donning his armor. Hermes knew, when he drank, that he talked too much, and it was apparent he had told the whore something of himself. Silently, he cursed his loose and foolish tongue.

"I am not going to London," he said coldly. "I am moving on."

"Moving on? Where?"

He cast her a long, hard stare. "On."

She would not let his surly answer deter her. "To the north is Worchester, Hereford, and Cumbria," she said. "I believe you told me your father resides in the north. Will you see him?"

"I told you that I would not tell you again to leave. Must I make good on my promise?"

"I *am* leaving, m'lord," she insisted. "I was simply making conversation of things we have already spoke of whilst donning my clothing."

"You're dressed now."

The whore had seen enough harsh, bitter men to know that he would never let her in to his harsh, bitter world. All of the kind words in the world would not open his hardened heart, and she knew their association was at an end.

Disappointed, she turned for the door.

"I hope you find what you are looking for, Sir Hermes," she said softly. "'Tis a terrible thing to be so angry and bitter at the world."

His jaw twitched. "I am not looking for anything. And I am who I am."

She opened the door, pausing in the darkness. The orange glow from the hearth barely lit her face as she gazed at the man who cried tearlessly and didn't even know it.

"Aye, you're looking for something. We all are." She began to close the door, very softly. "When you find it, you'll know."

The door closed. Her words echoed in his head. He paused in dressing, his head coming up, very slowly, as if he was just coming to realize what she had said.

When you find it, you'll know...

CHAPTER TWO

HERMES HATED NORTHUMBERLAND. He always had. A bleak province far away from the heart of England. Winters were hell here; he'd spent enough here to know. Practically his entire life, as his father was the garrison commander of Northwood Castle, a mighty bastion that sat along the Scots border. That was where he'd learned the art of healing, from his grandfather who had been both a great knight and a great healer.

A man Hermes missed every single day.

Hermes had endured the usual childhood and young adulthood. He'd trained with his father and grandfather, and then he'd married at the appropriate time. A young lass, daughter of a lesser nobleman, but a young lass he'd been quite in love with.

Until that had ended in tragedy.

He couldn't save her.

After that, he'd worked hard to forget her and everything that had ever mattered to him. His father had sent him to serve the king, simply to get him away from the bad memories, and rather than serve as a knight, he'd served as a physic to the king's troops. There had been no finer physic in the royal army; not a boast, but a fact. Everyone had wanted Hermes de Norville to heal their ailments or set their limbs. And he'd had a surgery ratio that was astonishing: one out of every three of his invasive surgery patients lived.

Sitting at a small, rotted table in small, rotted tavern in a dirty town deep in Cumbria, Hermes took another drink of his ale and darkly pondered the past. A past that consumed his present and his future, for he could do or say or think nothing else. It wasn't enough that his wife had died shortly after the birth of his twins of a raging fever and he could do nothing to help her, but he had been foolish enough to fall for another woman three years later who had been in love with another man. He had never blamed the woman, for she could not help whom she loved. But the bitterness Hermes felt, though he hadn't realized it at first, had overwhelmed him. Fortune did not favor him in the least. And God apparently had a personal vendetta against him.

"A drink, my friend?"

A voice pierced his bitter reflections. Hermes didn't react for a moment; he was hoping that if he ignored the question, the asker would go away. But a man planted his fat body on a seat beside him instead.

"I was asking to buy you one, my friend, not beggar one." The man was dressed in the fine robes of a merchant, with a big, round face and ruddy cheeks. "Would you permit me?"

"I can buy my own drink."

The man's jovial expression didn't waver. "I've no doubt, my good man," he said. "I was merely intending to celebrate my excellent fortune and, even though you are a stranger, was hoping you would join me. Good fortune is something everyone should celebrate, don't you think?"

Hermes couldn't help but give him an icy stare; there was no good fortune in the world, at least for him. Now was not the time for anyone, least of all a stranger, to be asking him that question. Taking his mug and the pitcher of ale that filled it, he left the bar and found himself a table in the corner. The merchant was puzzled at Hermes's behavior but not deterred; he simply turned to the next man at the bar, asked him the same question, and found a willing drinking comrade.

The room was warm, growing warmer still as the afternoon progressed into evening. Hermes wallowed in his alcohol as the room turned shades of orange and gold as the sun set. He found that if he drank enough, it dulled the gnawing pain in his chest long enough to afford some relief. He prescribed the same treatment for himself nearly every day, ignoring the fact that his health wasn't as good as it once had been. He tended to grow exhausted more easily, and three times during the winter he'd come down with a terrible cough. But he didn't particularly care that he was ruining his health; he didn't have anything, or anyone, to live for, so what did it matter?

The hour of dinner came, and the patrons of the inn feasted on huge trenchers of mutton. Hermes continued to drink while they ate, his red-rimmed eyes watching the room like a cat watching a mouse. He could hold his liquor well, and in spite of his inebriation, his focus was amazingly alert. What he was watching for was anyone's guess, including his own; his years of formal training as a knight left him with the innate sense that danger was always lurking about, and he kept dutifully vigilant even when he was drunk. His back was to the wall so no one could sneak up behind him.

"There is no reason to be alone on such a fine eve as this." The merchant was back with a huge container of ale. He plopped a full cup on the table before Hermes and sat heavily in the chair next to him. "In fact, I forbid it. And you, my surly friend, cannot ruin my pleasure. I say that we will drink to the birth of my fat, healthy grandson."

Hermes was on the brink of physically tossing the merchant from the table. But the moment the man mentioned the birth, Hermes felt himself relent. He couldn't fault the merchant his joy at a new life. Hermes himself could easily remember his own joy at the birth of his children, and based on that fact alone, he permitted the man the pleasure of his company, if for only a few moments.

"Very well," he said, taking the fresh cup of ale offered, and downed the contents in two long swallows. "To your grandson I will drink."

The fat merchant poured more ale into the emptied cup. "Children are the only true joy God gives us. Do you have children of your own, my friend?"

Hermes's face was expressionless. After a long, deliberative moment, he drank the second cup of ale and watched as the merchant poured him more. "I have two; a son and a daughter."

The merchant's face lit with glee. "Magnificent! Then you know well of what I speak."

The alcohol, as usual, loosened Hermes's tongue. "I do. Healthy children are our greatest gifts from the Almighty."

"How old are your children, my friend?"

"They have seen six years."

"And they live with you?"

The merchant was referring to this dark, dirty little town. Hermes shook his head. "I do not live here."

"Not in this dismal little town?"

"Nay."

"I see," the merchant said, pouring more ale. "Then you are a traveling man, like myself? Where is your home?"

Hermes swirled the drink in his cup, his sky-blue eyes dark with reflection. "All of England."

"There is not one place where you lay your boots?"

"There used to be. No longer."

"But what of the children?"

Hermes took a long drink of the deep, gold ale. "My mother has taken care of them since the death of my wife."

The merchant sobered, watching Hermes as the man finished off his fourth full cup. The pain, usually kept so tightly bottled inside, found an outlet through the alcohol.

"My condolences, my friend," the merchant said quietly. "I lost my sister in childbirth many years ago. Though it is not the same as losing your wife, still, I sympathize with your pain. 'Tis a noble death for a woman."

Hermes set a cup down and ran his hands over his face, feeling the stubble scratch his palms. "There is nothing noble about death," he muttered. 'Tis an instrument of destruction for those left behind."

"Destruction?"

"It destroys the soul of those left only with a memory."

The merchant topped off Hermes's cup again. The ale had been for celebration only moments earlier; now it was for easing the anguish. "You miss her?"

Hermes thought a moment. "I am angry with her for what has happened since she left. Had she not died, I would not have known the life I know now."

A whore came around, and the merchant chased her away. He was suddenly protective of his hostile new friend. "She did not die by choice," he said seriously. "But the life you live is indeed by your choice. Perhaps you should not seek to blame others for your misery."

It was not in Hermes's nature to flare in anger. He was always cool, remarkably so. He thought on the merchant's words even though the instinct to respond furiously was strong. Still, he could not refute the wisdom. It was perhaps the most prudent advice he had heard in a long while. Even if he was drunk, and miserable to boot, Hermes was not a fool.

"Congratulations on your legacy." He couldn't think of anything else to say. "If you will now leave me in peace, I would be grateful."

The merchant would obey his wishes. He rose from his chair, his piercing eyes studying Hermes intently. "Take heart, Sir Knight.

Happiness will come to you when you least expect it."

Hermes looked up at him. "Happiness? What makes you think I am seeking happiness?"

"Do you like being miserable?"

"Possibly."

The merchant chuckled softly. "You're not a good liar. Truth is your strength, my friend."

"How do you know that? You don't know me in the least."

"I can see it in your eyes."

He turned and left. Hermes watched him wander from the room and disappear through an open door leading out to the stables beyond. He was still pondering their conversation when the front door to the inn suddenly flew open. Two large, dirty women entered, pulling a smaller woman between them. There was quite a fight going on and the patrons of the tavern began to shout and place wagers on who would win the struggle.

"We've caught her!" one of the larger women shouted. "The Angel of Death! *We've caught her!*"

Their cries caught the attention of everyone in the room, including Hermes. Someone raced up to the smaller, trapped woman and pulled the hood from her head, exposing cascades of luscious auburn hair. It tumbled about wildly as she fought against the two that held her, but suddenly there were more people closing in and she lashed out a foot, catching one of her persecutors in the shin. The fat woman howled and released her hold.

Terrified, like a trapped animal, the small-boned woman yanked herself free of the other woman gripping her. Propelling herself forward, she was easily restrained by two men who had moved to block the other door. One grabbed her around the chest, but she went limp, like a child, and slithered from his grasp. Evading grabbing, harmful hands, she stumbled over a chair and scooted across a couple of tables, ducking under another table when a big man with dirty hands came too close. They were all chasing her about the room like fools, howling at their game and determined to catch her.

Hermes seemed to be the only person in the entire inn that wasn't resolved to race around her like an idiot. He sat back and observed the upheaval with disinterest until the woman came near his table. Through his alcohol-hazed eyes, he caught a glimpse of her face and thought, for a moment, that she looked strangely familiar, though he couldn't imagine where they had met before. Still, he couldn't shake the feeling that only seemed to grow stronger.

The struggling woman tripped over her long skirts and fell to the floor. Up until that moment, she had shown astonishing agility. But she was unable to recover her feet fast enough and the horde was on her, holding her fast. The woman struggled and kicked, but she was no match for the crowd. Hermes would have simply left them to their business had someone not struck the woman across the face, and she was suddenly looking in his direction.

Help me!

Hermes stared at her. A bolt of shock surged through him and the cup he was holding clattered to the ground. Her deep green eyes gazed at him with terror. Before he even realized what he was doing, he was on his feet and moving toward her.

"Surely the townsfolk can find better sport than chasing a frightened young woman about." His voice was deep and controlled. "Release her or you might find yourselves victim to her angry husband."

The people of the inn were dirty, earthy human beings being held together by their common ignorance. They stared at Hermes like he was a golden beacon among the slime.

"Do ye know who she is?" said a woman with missing teeth who had trapped her. "She's the Angel—"

Hermes cut her off. "I know, the Angel of Death. But I can hardly imagine that a woman such as this has committed such evil that you would brand her Satan's messenger." He gestured to the men holding the frightened woman. "Release her."

A man with wildly matted dark hair snorted. "Says who?"

Hermes fixed him in the eye. "Sir Hermes de Norville, son of Hector de Norville, commander of Northwood Castle, and grandson to William de Wolfe, the Earl of Warenton. Need I go on?"

"The Earl of Warenton?" the man repeated. "Northumberland?"

"Aye." Hermes's gaze was steady, though with all of the alcohol, he was feeling anything but steady. "I can bring the entire Scots border down around your ears, so listen carefully and heed my warning."

The man nodded slowly; in fact, all of the frenzied activity in the room seemed to have come to a halt. Everyone was staring at Hermes with new respect.

"William de Wolfe," said the man. "We know of his reputation, even here. Are you his heir?"

Hermes felt a stab at that question. At one time, he might have taken the man's head off for asking. But that was when he was young and had every reason to be bitter about it. Now, with the passing of years, it was simply a bitterness he had learned to live with, along with everything else. "Nay," he replied calmly. "I am no one's heir, not even my father's. I am…no one."

The atmosphere of the room was odd; it was obvious they admired Hermes by virtue of his family and relations to the church. But there was extreme confusion with regards to the wench—should they release her because he had asked? If they didn't, perhaps all of Northwood Castle, not to mention anything belonging to William de Wolfe's properties, might punish them. No one wanted to risk the wrath of the de Wolfe family; they had a mighty army with which to protect England from the Scots barbarians.

An army that could easily march to Cumbria.

The townsfolk looked around at each other, torn by their confusion.

"M'lord," the man with the matted hair said respectfully, even though he still held the frightened lady with an iron grip. "This…this lady is a curse upon our village. Ye understand that we must punish her."

Hermes looked at the lowered, tousled head, realizing that her hair wasn't dark auburn, as he had originally thought. It was lighter, with fascinating shades of brown and chestnut, red and gold running through it. It was the most miraculous color he had ever seen.

A strange feeling of familiarity gripped him again, and he moved toward her, placing the fingers of his right hand on her chin. Lifting her face, he gazed into deep, clear green eyes.

"Is this true?" he asked. "Have you committed crimes against these people?"

She shook her head unsteadily. "I have not, m'lord," she whispered, a breathy, sweet sound. "I am innocent."

She was a beautiful creature. Hermes couldn't stop staring at her creamy skin and rose-colored lips. "Then why would they say terrible things against you?"

She struggled to give him an answer, looking around at those imprisoning her, terrified to tell him the truth. "I came to town to gain aid from my brother," she told him. "He's…ill."

"The Dragon himself!" one woman howled. "He has sent her to destroy us!"

The reaction was instantaneous: the crowd surged, grumbling and crossing themselves. Hermes glanced around, struck curious by their response. But he also knew, at that instant, that he had to get this woman out of the tavern or surely she would meet her demise. Whoever the Dragon was, it was obvious that there was no love for him, and the fact that this woman was related to him did her no favors.

Hermes should have simply kept to his own business. But the longer he stared at the green-eyed lady, the more he knew he could not leave her to their mercy.

"Who is the Dragon?" He directed the question at those holding her.

They were all eager to answer, but only the loudest were heard. "The master of Castle Draygon," the toothless old woman told him.

"Castle Draygon? Where is this place?"

Several fingers pointed. "To the north," the woman answered. "Seated on a hill amongst the darkness of the haunted forest. The walls are built with bones. The entire place is cursed, it is!"

He didn't believe in dragons or hauntings and was beginning to find this conversation annoying. "And a dragon lives there?"

"The Dragon of Draygon!" They all clucked and shook their heads. "Pure evil, I say. And she's his messenger of death!"

Hermes repressed the urge to roll his eyes at their ignorance. Instead, he turned to the frightened lady among the rabble. "What's your name?" he asked her.

Her lower lip was trembling, her cheek red from the slap she had been given. But she answered him strongly. "The Lady Ana Paloma Catrine de la Pare, m'lord."

"That's quite a mouthful. Do I have to call you by your full name every time I address you?"

She could see the humor in his eyes, and it startled her. "Nay, m'lord. Catrine will suffice."

The corner of his mouth twitched and his eyes glimmered. He realized at that moment that there was no way he was going to leave her here for the vultures to feed upon her sweet flesh.

He turned to the grumbling crowd. "What crimes has this woman committed against you?" he demanded.

The people looked at each other, shoving and whispering, until the woman with missing teeth spoke again. "The Angel of death!" she shouted. "That is crime enough!"

"Has anyone ever seen her do anything against you?" he asked.

No one seemed to have an immediate answer. "Her family has cursed us!" someone shouted.

"But has this woman herself cursed you?"

It was apparent they were growing more confused and sullen; someone was actually *defending* her. Hermes leapt onto the nearest table, his big body as lithe as a cat. He faced the ignorant throng.

"If one person here can give me reason enough, I'll leave her to your justice," he announced. "But if I cannot be given a logical, convincing reason, then I will demand you release her. Well?"

They all looked around like stupid sheep, each waiting for the other to reply. A few people even turned away and went back to their meals. Hermes looked pointedly at the lady with missing teeth.

"Surely you can give me a reason," he said. "Has she murdered? Has she stolen? Has she maimed men or drained the blood of infants?"

The woman shook her head. "Yer an outsider," she grumbled. "Ye cannot know what the House of de La Pare has done tae us."

"Tell me, then."

"Horrible, unspeakable things."

"I'm listening."

The woman was silent a moment. Then she looked at Catrine and her expression seemed to take on a wounded countenance. "I've lived many years in this village," she said softly. "When I was a young woman, it was rumored that the lady of Castle Draygon was the most beautiful woman in all the land. Married though she was, men still came from miles to look upon her face. The Lord of Draygon was a jealous man and murdered the foolish suitors who came for his wife. He used their bones to build his walls. Then a bishop came from London to discover the truth of the happenings. 'Twould seem that one of the murdered suitors was a nephew to King Henry, though no one could be sure."

"And?"

"And the bishop was murdered as well, and God cursed the House of Draygon as well as her vassals. Our children starve, if they are even born at all, and our farmers can hardly scratch out a living from the earth." She jabbed a finger at Catrine. "And *her* family is to blame. 'Twas her mother who did this tae us!"

The crowd loudly agreed. Hermes turned to Catrine, trapped like a beautiful bird among crows. It was difficult to reason with a legend, no matter how illogical or foolish it was. These people believed what they believed, and he knew there was no possibility he could reason with them. Being superstitious and ignorant only compounded the problem of what had once probably been the mere story of a beautiful woman with a jealous husband.

The situation was looking grim; he wasn't sure how he was going to free her from this stupid crowd without any bloodshed. He realized that he was most likely about to do battle, and he mentally prepared himself for what would undoubtedly be an ugly confrontation. Even though his body tensed, his mind searched for one last possible reason that these people might understand for a peaceful end.

But what he didn't consider was the fact that Catrine knew the situation as well. She'd spent her entire life being tormented by the peasants of the village and knew there would be no peace until her guts were spilled on the floor. She wasn't willing to take the chance that this noble knight could free her with logic.

She had to fight.

With a shriek, she threw her small body forward, jerking herself free from those holding her. Iin a panic, she raced around the room, dodging those who tried to recapture her. Soon the entire tavern was in an uproar as chairs toppled and tables were smashed. When she finally bolted through the door that led to freedom outside, Hermes leapt from the table and held up his hands before the crowd stampeded after her.

"Wait!" he commanded. "Let no one pursue her!"

The crowd pulsed and roared. Hermes unsheathed the sword from his side, wielding it in a threatening manner. He was fully willing to take the head of the first idiot who challenged him. At the sight of his mighty weapon, the townsfolk immediately tamed. They had no desire to battle the son of de Norville, for they had no doubt he would use the blade, and not one of them wished to die this night. An uneasy calm settled as they stared at each other, one knight against two dozen fools.

Hermes's expression was deadly serious. He held the sword in a defensive position for a moment longer before slowly bringing it to rest by his left thigh; being left-handed, he handled his sword differently than most, but it was by no means less deadly. In fact, he oft believed he had the advantage, as it usually threw his opponents off balance, as they were accustomed to battling right-handed men. One moment of confusion as all he needed.

"Ye let her get away!" the man with matted hair cried. "Now the curse will never be ended!"

Hermes's patience with these people was at an end. "Do you really believe it would be ended if you killed or tortured her? Of course not. She's not the root of the problem."

"Nay, she's not," the man replied. "But she does the bidding of the Dragon. And he is the soul of the curse."

"What do you mean?"

The crowd grew quiet, uncertain. The dirty, matted man spoke. "'Twas said that before the bishop died, he asked God to curse the firstborn of the lady of Castle Draygon. Through him, the curse is carried on. If he dies without an heir, then the spell will be broken."

"And you intend to get to him through his sister?"

The people nodded, determined and frightened at the same time. Hermes scratched his head and re-sheathed his sword. He didn't know why he should involve himself, but something in those terrified eyes spoke to a part of him he'd kept long-buried and carefully hidden. He couldn't shake the feeling of familiarity, either. Besides, he had nothing better to do with himself at the moment, and he almost felt an appeal in the distraction. It didn't hurt things in the least that Lady Catrine de la Pare was hauntingly beautiful.

"Very well," he finally said. "I shall make you a proposal. Since I allowed your Angel of Death to escape, I say it is only right that I recapture her. But in doing so, I intend to discover the evidence behind this curse. If there is no curse, then you will leave the woman and her brother in peace. But if I see indication of something evil at work, then I shall destroy them myself and raze the castle. Do we have a bargain?"

The crowd looked at each other, some nodding, some shaking their heads. They couldn't decide if that was a fair deal. They'd come to loathe the occupants of Castle Draygon for so long that to think there was possibly no basis for their hatred was confusing. What if there was no curse? What if there was nothing up on that barren hill but a dilapidated castle and a destitute, once-noble family? If that were the case, then they'd no longer have any common hatred. Then who would they blame for their suffering?

Finally, the man with the matted hair spoke. "Ye're an honored knight?"

"Of the finest order."

He was silent a moment longer; it was obvious that he was having difficulty releasing his sense of vengeance to another. "As ye say, then," he said slowly. "See for yourself, since none of us has the skill or courage to do it. But if you kill 'em, bring their heads to us. We want tae know that the devil and his sister are dead."

Hermes breathed out a small sigh of relief; he hadn't thought they would agree with him. Quickly, so they could not change their minds, he fled the inn. His gray charger with the coal-black mane and tail was waiting for him at the livery behind the tavern, and together the two of them galloped up the road, just ahead of the storm that blew in over the countryside and lit the sky with its fury.

On the rolling thunder, he could swear he heard her voice, and it only moved him faster.

…help me!

CHAPTER THREE

E YES WERE WATCHING from the tower.

The thunder rumbled across the sky and rain splattered on the sill of the narrow lancet window. Far below on the narrow, winding road, a tiny figure struggled against the elements. The wind was vicious and unbalancing as the tiny shape passed beneath the double portcullis entry and into the mud-filled bailey. The eyes lost sight of the figure when it was consumed by the keep, but the disappearance was momentary. It would only be a matter of minutes before he saw the figure again, sure as life, before him.

He had been expecting her.

Shortly, there was a knock on the door of the dreary tower chamber. Slowly, the splintered oaken door opened and a head appeared. Fearful eyes gazed hesitantly about the room. When she saw him, she quickly entered the room and closed the door behind her.

"Forgive me," she said, through she did not sound remorseful in the least. "I could not complete my task."

He reached out a gnarled hand, touching her hooded head. She froze when she saw the bony fingers, thinking that perhaps he would try to gouge her eyes out. When dealing with him, one never knew what to expect. But the wicked, long fingers merely lingered on the material a moment, caressing it, before finally pulling it away from her head. Glimmering chestnut hair appeared, and he touched it suggestively. She pulled away from him as discreetly as she could manage, though her disgust was evident.

He ignored it.

"My fair Catrine," he said, the voice twisted and raspy. "How have you failed me, my sweet?"

She wasn't afraid of him, though she hated being near him. Her hurried manner was not born out of nerves, but of a distinct desire to be away from his presence. The quicker she said what needed to be said, the sooner she would leave this horrid place filled with phials and creatures and strange smells.

It was an abomination, just as he was.

"The peasants captured me," she explained in her soft, sweet voice. "I barely escaped with my life."

His thin, dry lips smiled. "But escape you did," he said. "How did you manage?"

"A knight," she said quietly, her magnificent green eyes suddenly distant as she thought on the broad, blond-haired man who had spoken so eloquently in her defense. She hadn't given him much thought until this moment, and now, she found she could hardly focus on anything else. He had been so...*beautiful.* "He...he distracted the villeins and allowed me to escape."

The smile vanished and the eyes looked at her with sudden hostility. "And you thanked him with your charms, no doubt?" he croaked. "Your luscious virgin body in his capable hands? Is that it? You're a damnable trollop in the image of your mother."

She remained calm in the face of his insult. "I did not have the chance to thank him at all. I had to flee for my life."

He couldn't decide whether he believed her. She was cursed with all of the faults and characteristics of a woman, from her overt beauty to her delicate mannerisms. Everything he found foul and revolting, he found in her, and it nauseated him. She was a vile creature too smart for her own good. Or was that, perhaps, the exact description of himself? He could not be sure where his own evil characteristics ended, and her sweet ones began. His malignancy flowed onto her until they were part of the same rancorous mold.

"So, you were able to escape with this knight's help," he said, proud that he was able to calm himself so capably. "But it does not excuse your failure. You must go back."

Her deep green eyes flashed angrily for a moment. But just as quickly, she cooled the heated surge. "I cannot go back. Not for a while, anyway. If they catch me again—"

"If they catch you again, it will be your own stupid fault."

"If I go back, they will disembowel me."

"You must go back. Simply do not get caught."

Catrine sighed heavily, knowing that to refuse would be futile. She nodded reluctantly, though she did not relish the idea of returning to the village. But it was the same trip she made every full moon, and each time the threat of capture grew. The townsfolk, not as ignorant as one would think, had come to anticipate her visit. Even though she varied the time of day and night that she went, still, nowadays there was always someone watching.

She sighed again, a delicate noise amidst the evil and darkness of the tower chamber. "Perhaps at dawn one day from now," she said. "I'll go before they awaken from their night's sleep."

"Wise," he agreed. "Do as you have done before. Put the ingredients directly in the well."

She nodded, perhaps a bit wearily. "I know."

He smiled as she rose and went for the door. She was a petite thing with fragile bones and a tiny waist. But her appearance belied her strength; she was as healthy as an ox. He'd never known her to be sick a day in her life, unlike himself. And the hair, hanging down to her buttocks in a silken cascade of waves, taunted him. She was an obscene creature.

Just like her mother.

He'd long ago decided that.

"Good lass," he said encouragingly. "Be obedient. It will keep the curse away from your dear brother."

She paused at the door, her gaze falling about the decrepit room at its contents. He fit quite comfortably amidst the squalor. She could only pray that she wouldn't end up like him some day. She wondered if there was truly any hope that she would be different.

The door closed, and he was left alone.

CHAPTER FOUR

ASTLE DRAYGON WAS the most formidable, bleakest, darkest, and eeriest place he had ever seen. And he had seen a good many dark, eerie places.

Hermes came to a halt on the road, his sky-blue eyes studying the structure intently; it sat on the top of an outcropping of dark, rocky hills, the stone of the castle itself hewn from the surrounding land and of the same dark gray color. Outlined against the stormy sky, the silhouette came into sharp focus every time the black clouds lit with streaks of lightning. The rain was pounding and the wind howling, and Hermes had no idea how long he actually stood there, watching. But the mere sight of Castle Draygon gave him a bad feeling in the pit of his stomach.

He shook himself, cursing his own foolishness. Maybe the tales of the village idiots had affected him more than he thought. Yet he could see where they imagined that the devil himself took residence in this place; it was truly hellish. Spurring his charger forward, he mounted the rocky, narrow road that led up the hill. The rain was brutal, and it seemed to take forever to near the top, and he sensed that, perhaps from his own imagination, the closer he drew, the worse the weather became.

He looked up, straining to catch a glimpse of life from the place; the damp stone walls were black with wet, and there was no light originating from within whatsoever. The structure was dark and lifeless, and as Hermes drew near, he found himself taking in the awesome spectacle of the twenty-five-feet perimeter walls. Obviously, the castle was built to withstand a siege of epic proportions, and he could only shake his head and wonder what army, so strong and mighty here in the wilds of Cumbria, could be such a horrendous threat.

The horse slipped in the mud, nearly pitching him off. The angle of the road was steep and uneven; it crept sharply upward toward the massive portcullis, which looked like a vicious mouth with great iron fangs ready to devour whoever passed beneath it. For safety's sake, Hermes dismounted the steed and led him the rest of the way through the sludge and pouring rain.

The closer Hermes drew to the open portcullis, the more impressive it became—there was no drawbridge or moat, unneeded because of the ridiculously high walls, merely a massive opening wide enough for an army to pass through. Furthermore, there weren't any gates to seal the opening; the portcullis was to serve as the only barrier. With as large as it was, it was an imposing barrier indeed, and Hermes knew that the iron barricade was stronger than any wooden structure could possibly be.

As he neared the jagged edges of the open grate, a great strike of lightning illuminated the walls of the fortress. He almost shielded his eyes because he was so accustomed to the darkness. But the brief flash was all he needed to see what precisely lay before him. He came to a halt, fixed to the spot and unable to move. He couldn't believe what he had just witnessed in that one instant, and he stood still, waiting for another bolt of illumination to confirm his first impression.

A few moments later the lightning struck again, and he was faced with the horror of horrors: lining the entrance of the massive black structure were the carcasses of countless dead animals. But embedded in the walls themselves were bones.

Hundreds of skulls and bones.

Hermes stared at the gruesome collage. He could have never had imagined anything this horrible, even in his worst nightmare. There were rows and rows of them, most mere skeletons, and he gazed at them in disgust and confusion. So many questions came to mind: Why where they here? Why weren't they buried in consecrated ground instead of being left to rot in the walls of a dark, sinister castle?

The rain came down, pounding his disbelieving eyes, and Hermes had to turn away; he couldn't look at the sight anymore. It was bad even for him. His gaze turned once again to the great, dark walls, and his feelings of dread deepened. No wonder the peasants were so fearful of this place. Were he not the logical sort, he might have been fearful of it, too. But at this moment, he realized he was mostly aggrieved.

The entry tunnel leading through the wall was at least twelve feet in length, the precise width of the wall. There was a huge, toothy portcullis on both ends, but neither gate was in working order. They'd long since been damaged. He wasn't quite sure what to expect upon entering the bailey and tried to keep calm about it.

Any more dead bodies and he might surely burn this evil place down.

Much to his relief, there were no bones waiting for him; in fact, his first reaction to the bailey was that it was a tiny, empty thing. Barely enough to house a dozen knights. But it took him a moment to realize that he was only gazing at the outer bailey. The inner bailey, as he discovered by passing through yet another passageway set within a massive inner wall, was much more impressive.

In truth, he'd never seen anything like it.

Hermes stood there a moment, inspecting the great area where an army of a thousand could easily be amassed. It was a wide, uneven plain that was incredibly vacant for all its size. Through the pounding rain, he could see the foot soldiers' quarters in an outcropping of small, crumbling structures braced against the inner wall. They looked as if they hadn't been occupied in years. To the right was the massive keep, towering five stories above his head with only small lancet windows for ventilation. Jutting from the south side of the keep was an incredibly tall turret, the tip of its pointed roof disappearing into the ominous clouds above.

Hermes stared up at it, shielding his eyes from the rain and thinking that this entire place was meant for something very, very big. He'd never seen such a massive structure this far from London, aside from his father's castle. Northwood was massive and wide, spread out over several acres and designed to house hundreds of troops to protect against the Scots. But Castle Draygon was impressive by sheer height; everything from the protective walls to the keep was meant for the sky. Hermes found himself comparing it to the Tower of Babel.

Maybe it really was *evil.*

The tower, however, was apparently empty. How could a place this size be empty? Hermes wandered into the bailey and tethered his horse beneath one of the crumbling shelters. The inner bailey was slick with mud, water running down the walls in torrents as he made his way toward the entrance of the keep. Lightning flared again and illuminated the ghostly black walls, and he half expected to see more dead bodies. But the stone walls were empty and the entrance to the magnificent keep was strangely understated. It was just a few steps and a door, hardly more. Even the door, from what he could see, was missing. He was about to step inside when a cry stopped him.

"Aux aremes!"

The shout pierced the rumble of the rain, and, startled, Hermes instinctively went for his sword. *To arms!* was a battle cry he had heard many times. His weapon was leveled defensively as a man leapt through the door, splashing into a huge puddle of mud with both feet. His rusted broadsword waved crazily in the rain and wind, slashing violently as he rent a wild path into the bailey.

Hermes tensed as he prepared to fight, and he was quite puzzled when the man danced right past him. A huge, heavy cross hung around his neck. Yet he skipped skillfully across the bailey, fighting opponents Hermes could not see. He was yelling in French, and it was apparent that he was determined to do battle.

Hermes watched the man lithely dance about and couldn't help but scratch his head. He had been positive the man was coming for him, preparing to defend Castle Draygon against an intruder. But Hermes continued to go unnoticed as the man fought ferociously across the bailey, engaging in mortal combat with nothing more than the storm. He never showed sign of fatigue, nor did he acknowledge any living creature. He skirted Hermes's charger without fear as the horse nipped and stomped at him, inherently roused by the sword and shouting, before fighting his way back into the keep.

Hermes followed him. The interior of Draygon was icy and smelled of rot. It was as dark inside as it was outside, and Hermes mostly found his way down the black corridor by feeling the walls and listening to the shouts of the fighting man. A couple of times his probing hands drew across something damp and slick, but he never questioned what it might have been. In truth, he didn't want to know.

His eyes grew accustomed to the near-complete darkness, and he could see that there was a very little light emerging from a doorway ahead. He could hear the fighting man and see his shadow dance on the walls up ahead. Cautiously, Hermes slowed when he came to the lit doorway, his eyes searching the room beyond. It had once been a foyer of sorts—a huge broken iron chandelier hung from the impossibly tall ceiling, and a winding stairway hugged the wall.

It was an interesting room, cylindrical in shape, and the fire came from a huge hearth located near the stairs. There was also a wardrobe of sorts, a massive piece of furniture that was scarred and worn, standing forlornly opposite the hearth. Hermes hung back in the doorway, his sword still drawn, and watched the fighting man as he lunged and struck at unseen forces.

"Coup de maître!"

The man struck out, landing what would have been a magnificent blow had he been fighting a visible opponent. He withdrew quickly, pretended to wipe the blood from his sword, and sheathed it at his side. Hermes sank back into the shadow of the doorway as the man, suddenly calm and with very much the military protocol, marched across the room and directly into the wardrobe. Throwing open the door, he stepped inside and closed himself in.

The room fell eerily still. Hermes stood a moment, waiting for the fighting man to come hurtling out of the wardrobe again, but he was met only with silence. In fact, he couldn't identify one solitary sound. Not even heavy breathing from the wardrobe, which would have been understandable, given the exertion the fighting man had just produced. Carefully, Hernes stepped into the once-grand room, his senses heightened. His instincts told him there was no danger in wait, but his warrior's senses refused to let him re-sheathe his sword. He stood in the middle of the round chamber, looking about, until his gaze came to rest on the dilapidated wardrobe. After a moment, he let his guard down long enough to shake his head with confusion.

"God's bones," he muttered. "What kind of freakish place is this?"

Only the echo of his soft voice answered him. Driven by curiosity, he walked over the wardrobe and knocked on it. He simply couldn't help himself; the crazy fighting man seemed to be the only inhabitant of this massive place. But there was no answer to the knock, and Hermes carefully opened the door. The fighting man was upright, leaning against the wardrobe wall and sleeping very carefully. He didn't even stir when Hermes poked him. Shaking his head, Hermes closed the door and sheathed his sword.

"What kind of freakish place *is* this?" he demanded again.

It was the last conscious thought he had as a sharp pain to the back of his head brought him to his knees. Everything was spinning wildly, and stars danced before his eyes. But he had the presence of mind to unsheathe his sword and roll onto his back, raising the sword upright to protect himself. A large piece of wood came crashing down atop his sword, but the blade was so sharp that it virtually hacked the wood in two. His attacker swung the wood at him again, this time with a very feminine-sounding growl, and the wood splintered.

Hermes's senses were muddled, but he heard the high-pitched shriek and decided to play a hunch. *"Catrine!"* he said quickly. "Don't be afraid. I've not come to harm you, truly!"

She swung the broken pieces at him. He deflected them easily with the sword. "Catrine," he said again, dodging a splintered projectile. "Catrine, listen to me. I mean you no harm. *Catrine!*"

Somewhere in the panic and fear, she heard his deep, urgent hiss, and the assault came to an unsteady end. The room was so dark that it made it difficult to see, but he could hear her heavy breathing. The broken wood hit the floor with a loud thud, and suddenly she was on her knees beside him, her eyes wide with shock.

"You!" she whispered. "It's…*you!*"

Hermes lay on his back like an upended turtle. His sword was still up, his body frozen in a defensive position as his blue eyes stared at her. God, she was even more beautiful than he had remembered.

"Aye, 'tis me," he replied weakly. "God's bones, you've a wicked blow. Did you intend to pummel me to death?"

She looked bewildered. "I…I didn't recognize you with your helm on." She grabbed him by the armor and yanked him into a sitting position. "What are you doing here? Why have you followed me?"

She was still holding on to him, and he let her. He was so close to her that for a moment, he was actually speechless; gazing into those deep green eyes was enough to make him forget every conscious thought. They swallowed him whole, giving him a warmth and giddiness that he'd never known. Hermes realized he would have been quite content to stare into those miraculous eyes forever.

He knew those eyes.

"I did not follow you," he said, trying to determine whether it was her gaze or the knock on the head making his stomach jump about so crazily. "I came to…help."

"Help?" she repeated, as if she had never heard the word. "What do you mean?"

He swallowed hard, feeling very flushed and hot. Something was either seriously wrong with him or this woman had an effect on him like no other; when was the last time he had actually *blushed*?

"When you came to the inn, you said you were looking for help for your ill brother," he said, rather pleased that excuse had come to him so easily. "I'm a physic."

She looked dubious. But she also looked afraid, and he hoped it wasn't because she was afraid of him. She let go of his armor and rocked back on her heels, eyeing him. Then she glanced about, looking up the stairs into the darkness as if searching for someone. She seemed to stare into the dark for a very long time.

"You shouldn't be here," she finally whispered. "You must leave."

"But you said your brother needed help."

She shook her head. "Not…not anymore," she said, rising to stand. "Please, Sir Knight, you must leave now."

He rose shakily, his head swimming. Sheathing his sword, he faced her. "You're not making any sense," he said. "You came to town for help, nearly got yourself killed in the process, and now that I offer my services, you refuse me?"

She took a step back from him, studying him just as he was studying her. She seemed so very hesitant. "You…you were truly a physic to King Henry?"

He nodded. "Indeed."

Catrine pondered his reply, looking at him a moment longer before looking up the stairs again, and this time, he followed her gaze. All he saw was blackness, and he wondered what, or whom, she was looking at. After several long, strangely tense seconds, she sighed and some of her resistance seemed to fade.

"I apologize that I've caused you so much trouble, first at the inn and now that you have come all the way to Draygon for nothing," she said. "But you must leave now, please. I do not require your help."

He took a step toward her, closing the distance between them. "Why?"

She took another step back, and he could see a faint pink hue coming to her cheeks. "Be…because you must."

"Give me a good reason or I will not leave."

Her pink cheeks deepened. "I need not give you a good reason. This is my home and I've asked you to leave."

"True enough. But what of your brother?"

"He doesn't need you."

"Do you insult my skill?"

"Of course not!"

She was backing up until she bumped into the wall and could back no further. Hermes kept advancing until he was standing toe-to-toe with her, gazing down at her sweet face and thinking he'd never in his life seen someone who looked so much like an angel. Not an Angel of Death, to be certain, but an angel of pure light.

Like it or not, he was infatuated.

"Then how can you be so sure I cannot help him?" he asked.

Catrine realized she was trapped, but she wasn't at all that uncomfortable with the fact. Truth be known, she felt warm and giddy and faint as he stood before her, a thin shift and shawl the only things separating her flesh from the cold armor pressed against her. When he looked at her with those beautiful, clear blue eyes, she couldn't think at all.

He seemed to suck the thoughts right from her.

"No one can help him," she heard herself say. "He is the way God has intended, and the miracle of potions or medicines cannot help him."

Hermes cocked an eyebrow. "I'm a fairly competent healer," he said. "Would you even say that before allowing me to try?"

His breath was hot on her face. Catrine closed her eyes, blocking out the sight of his magnificent features and praying that God gave her the strength to do what was best for them both. She imagined that telling him he was in great danger wouldn't make a difference to him; he was a knight, and an extremely capable one. He would simply look at it as a challenge. But she knew, from experience, that she had to convince him to leave or they would both be lost.

"Please," she murmured. "Please leave. You can do no good here."

She opened her eyes, and he was closer than she thought, their noses nearly touching. A wild tingling sensation ran through her body, making it difficult to breathe. A thousand pounds weighed on her chest until she could scarcely draw a breath. All she could see was his mouth, the smooth, even lips looming before her. They curved into a smile and came toward her, and with her last shred of control, she turned her head and they moved tenderly across her cheek.

Her hands came up, half pushing him, half pulling him. "Nay," she murmured. "You…mustn't. You must leave, please!"

Hermes was a man possessed. It was as if someone else had control of his mind and body, causing him to touch this woman without thought or remorse. It was so natural, so completely right, that he simply couldn't stop himself. He didn't *want* to stop himself. When his arms came up and he pulled her into his embrace, he swore at that moment that he'd never held sweeter.

"I'm not leaving," he whispered huskily. His lips had found a small, delicate ear, and he suckled the lobe. "And if I do, I'm taking you with me."

Her bones turned to water and she went limp in his arms. "How can you say that?"

"Very easily."

"But you're mad. You don't even know of me!"

"I don't need to."

She could not resist nor reply as he lifted her up, holding her fast against him. Her arms wound around his neck and her fingers slipped beneath the helm, preparing to lift it off. She had remembered the cropped reddish-blond hair and longed to run her hands over it. She didn't even know this man, yet she was so consumed with him that nothing else in the world seemed to matter until she dreamily opened her eyes.

And then she saw it.

A shadowed, hulking figure lingered at the top of the stairs, heavily muscled arms and legs distinctly outlined in the dim light. She could see his chest as it moved in and out, in and out, heaving with every breath. Catrine's eyes widened and she pulled back from Hermes, so quickly that she bumped her head on the wall behind her. He looked at her, confused and flushed, and was startled to see such fear in her eyes.

"Please," she said, grabbing him by the hand, yanking him toward the corridor leading out to the baileys. "We must go!"

Hermes was not a man to feel or show fear. It took quite a bit for him to work up into any level of anxiety. But Catrine was verging on hysteria, and he permitted her to lead him down the corridor, bumping into the walls in the blackness until they reached the outer bailey. He didn't want her to venture out into the rain, but she ignored his protests and pulled him out into the driving weather. Very quickly, she was soaked to the skin as she took him through the mud and water before catching sight of his tethered horse. She led him directly to the animal before releasing his hand.

Her hair was wet, stuck to her pink cheeks. Her deep green eyes were unnaturally bright against her white skin as she gazed at him, a longing in her expression that he could not describe, but he knew matched his own. There was a magnetism between them he couldn't begin to describe. The urge to kiss her was overwhelming, but his innate sense of logic superseded his lustful impulses.

For the moment, anyway.

"Why did we have to leave so quickly?" he asked, his voice as low and distant as the rumbling thunder. "What is in that place the frightens you so?"

She wasn't going to tell him anything. It went too deep, too far, for a stranger to comprehend. Even a stranger as smart and wonderful as him.

"Please," she murmured. "Go now. Don't ever come back."

He lifted his eyebrows. "Not bloody likely, lady."

She looked pained. "Don't be a fool. Can't you see that this place only means death for you?"

His expression was deadly serious. "I can see that it means death for *you* if you stay. Surely this gloom and evil will kill you." He took a step toward her, his eyes glittering. "Where do these dead bodies come from, Catrine? Who has put them here?"

Tears sprang to her eyes, and he was surprised; she didn't seem to be the crying sort. But considering the question, he could understand the response. She shook her head. "I...I cannot..."

"And that man who fights phantoms? Who is he?"

She shook her head again, unwilling to answer. "Go away," she said, turning her back to him. "Please, Sir Knight. I beg of you."

"My name is Hermes. You will call me Hermes and, someday, husband." He grabbed her, spinning her around to face him. "Do you comprehend me? I don't know what's going on in this evil place, but I won't permit you to be a lasting part of it."

Her teary eyes were wide with shock. "Surely you cannot be serious?"

"Why not? Are you already married?"

"No."

"Then I shall marry you."

She was at a loss. "But…*why*?"

"Because I want to."

A logical answer, one she could not argue with. Truth be known, she felt a tremendous amount of excitement at his statement. It was almost too good to imagine, her wildest dream that she never thought to come true. She shook her head again, overwhelmed by the mere thought.

"You're…you're mad!"

He smiled, a delicious gesture that revealed straight white teeth. "Perhaps," he said slowly. "What is your answer?"

She didn't know what to say. "I…I cannot give you one."

He reached for the reins of his stallion, throwing them up on the saddle. "Then I shall return tomorrow and ask your brother's permission," he said. "Surely he is the head of your household. And while I'm here, I shall tend his illness."

Her rosy lips were turning blue. "Nay," she gasped. "You mustn't!"

He ignored her distress and turned her in the direction of the keep. "Go inside now," he said. "'Tis freezing out here, and you'll catch your death. I would have my future wife alive and healthy."

She let him push her out into the mud and rain before her feet seemed able to move on their own. She was halfway across the bailey when she stopped and turned to him.

"I told you never to return, Sir Hermes. I meant it."

He simply smiled and mounted his horse. The charger plowed through the mud and rain, thundering across an inner bailey that had once known the feel of hooves very, very well. Catrine watched him go, knowing without a doubt it would not be the last she saw of him.

Hermes was equally as positive and feeling rather buoyant about it. But just outside of the massive portcullis, his charger slipped and sent the both of them hurtling down the steep, rocky hill. The stud broke his neck, and Hermes's last conscious thought as he slipped through the mud and rocks was that his broken neck lay not far behind. God was still apparently very much against him.

CHAPTER FIVE

"**H**E'S GONE NOW," she said softly, standing in the doorway. "I sent him away."

"Who was he?"

The voice rumbled from the blackness. The room was so very dark that it was difficult to see anything at all, but that was the way he wanted it. Catrine entered what had once been a grand chamber; it was a massive room with a great bed in the middle, the tatters of once-beautiful linens hanging from the mattress. An expensive rug nearly half the length of the room lay dirty and worn upon the cold stone, a mere shell of its former glory. Everything about the chamber spoke of days gone by that had been prosperous and splendid, but now it was simply an effigy of bad fortune.

And it smelled bad, like the stench of human bodies. Catrine's nose wrinkled at the rankness, and she shook off a sneeze. There was a small fire in the hearth, sending off more smoke than flame as she moved toward the center of the room. In the shadows, a hulking figure sat, awaiting her explanation.

"I went to the village today," she said. "The peasants captured me and surely would have killed me had the knight not intervened and saved my life.”

The figure grunted. “So, he followed you home?”

She shrugged uncomfortably. “I misled him.”

“How?”

A small, slender finger toyed with the shredded linen hanging from the bed canopy. “I was terrified when the villeins captured me. I knew they were going to kill me, so I made up a lie,” she said. “The knight…he was the only person not determined to murder me. He must be a visitor to the village, because I’ve never seen him nor even heard of a knight in these parts. In any case, when he intervened and asked my purpose in town, I told him that I was seeking him for my ill brother.”

“A foolish lie.”

“I know. But it was the only excuse I could think of.”

“But why would he come here?”

“He says he is a physic. He wanted to help you.”

The man in the shadows was silent. Then he snorted softly. “A knight-physic,” he murmured. “Lo, that I wish I could claim the title of knight as he does. What do you know of him?”

“Not much.”

“From what house does he hail?”

“De Norville,” she said. “His father is the commander of North-wood Castle and his grandfather was the Earl of Warenton, William de Wolfe. He is a former physic to the king.”

He seemed impressed. “Grandson of the Earl of Warenton,” he said softly. “A mighty knight. And mightily full of himself, I would wager.”

Even in the darkness, Catrine could see the sadness and bitterness on his distorted features, and her heart twisted with the familiar pity. “Though you did not complete your conventional training, you’re the most powerful warrior I’ve ever seen. Surely this knight is not greater than you.”

"He would say so, I am sure."

He sighed heavily and rose from his chair. He was a massive figure, tall and broad, exquisitely sculpted. But as the light from the fire fell on his form, it was not difficult to see why kept himself in darkness. He would have been deeply handsome had the curse not affected him with nodules all over his face, deforming his features. The same affliction was on his neck, chest, and down his back—bumps and sores that he had tried to cure, for many years, but these days he just covered it all up. But the dark green eyes that focused on Catrine were bright and beautiful; the torture of his affliction ran deeper than words could express.

Catrine had long grown accustomed to her brother's countenance. His childhood appearance had been normal enough until as a young man of fourteen, the nodules first appeared. He had been fostering at Berkeley Castle, but his master knight had a sister living in Cumbria who told him of the curse inflicted upon Castle Draygon by a murdered bishop. Not wanting to be part of any curse, imagined or otherwise, the Lord of Berkeley had sent the young squire home. His training incomplete, he returned home to find himself further plagued by the bumps that grew, and to a distraught and maddened father.

"Does the title 'sir' matter so much, Bennet?" Catrine asked softly. "You've inherited the barony from our father. Does the fact that you were never confirmed as a knight truly matter so much now?"

He paused, raking his big hand through his dark hair; it was soft, with a hint of a curl and auburn lights. "Nothing matters now," he muttered. "Did the beast in the tower see him?"

Catrine jaw flexed with disgust. "I do not know. I've not yet seen him to ask."

Bennet turned to her, his eyes grazing her. He knew how much she hated this life they found themselves living. But penitence, Bennet had long since learned, could be agonizing. Not strange that the children found themselves paying for the sins of their parents.

"Do not worry over it," he said. "You shall see him soon enough."

She sighed heavily, closing her eyes for a brief, painful moment. "God, I hate him," she whispered fervently. "Will this ever end, Bennet? Will we ever know the cessation of this torture?"

He shrugged. "I will not. But for you, I would hope someday."

Catrine opened her eyes, staring at the weak fire. A thought occurred to her, and the more she thought on it, the more unnerved she became. "Would…would a marriage release me from this hell, or would it simply drag my husband into our mire?"

He snorted. "Marriage? Christ, girl, where do you get such ideas?" he asked, pouring himself a cup of strong, tart wine, alcohol they fermented themselves from the berries and wild grapes that Catrine gathered. "For instance, where would you meet a prospective groom? Even if you did, we've nothing to offer him by the way of a dowry. All we have to offer is a damnable family curse and years of misery."

"You're saying that he would be cursed as well?"

"Anyone related to the damnable family would be."

Her delicate jaw twitched, and she refused to look at him. It seemed to her that he was ranting at her, though she knew in her heart that he was not. It was simply her brother's way to be brutally truthful.

"I appreciate your frankness, brother," she said quietly. "But in spite of your views, I think I've met a prospective bridegroom."

He looked at her, knowing exactly whom, and what, she meant. "Your noble knight?"

Catrine nodded, tight-lipped, waiting for him to laugh at her foolish hopes. "How long were you standing at the top of the stairs?" she asked.

"What do you mean?"

She turned to him. "When the knight was here," she clarified. "How long were you standing at the top of the stairs watching us?"

He was silent a moment. Taking a long drink of wine, he drained the cup and poured himself another.

"Long enough to see you melt within his embrace," he muttered.

She should have been embarrassed but found she was not. "You saw him touch me, yet you did not kill him?" she said, shaking her head. "That does not make sense. You've imprisoned every intruder to Draygon that I can recall. Our bowels are lined with the unfortunate living who became the fortunate dead. Why did you not capture him as well, for putting his hands on me, no less?"

Bennet took a long, deep breath. "Would you prefer that I capture him so that he would always stay here, with you?"

"Of course not."

"Then why question my mercy?"

She grabbed his arm, fixing him in the eye. He pulled from her grasp simply for the fact that he didn't want her infected with his ooze. "Because it's unlike you to show mercy, Bennet," she said. "They call you the Dragon for a very good reason—you don't *show* mercy."

He stared at her for a long moment. Very slowly, he set down his half-full cup of wine and wandered to the one of the three long lancet windows cut into the wall of his chamber. Outside, the storm was abating and a full moon played hide-and-seek behind the black clouds. He felt the ghostly moonlight caress his face as the cold breeze eased the constant fire of his disease. As he enjoyed the marginal relief, he thought on his sister's words carefully. It wasn't in his nature to keep anything from her, nor was it in his nature not to tell her the truth.

"My eyesight is as sharp as a hawk's," he said quietly.

"I know," Catrine said.

"I can see in the dark better than any man alive."

"That is because you live in the dark, Bennet," she said, her voice soft. "You see things most of us cannot."

He was quiet a moment. "I saw your face as the knight was holding you, Catrine."

She was torn between apprehension and wonder. "What do you mean?"

He gazed from the window, seeing the beauty of the clearing sky and relishing in it. It wasn't often that nights here were as beautiful as this. "How were you feeling at that moment?"

She thought back, and it was not hard to recall the emotions. But she wasn't sure what answer he was seeking. "Well…excitement, I suppose."

"Is that how you would describe it?"

She thought harder and felt her limbs turn warm and liquid at the mere idea of the knight's powerful arms around her. It was an enveloping heat that caused her lightheadedness and heaviness at the same time, and she smiled as the wonderous feelings swamped her.

"Nay," she whispered. 'Twas far more than that."

"What, then?"

"Unadulterated happiness, delirious rapture, overwhelming joy."

He turned to her in the darkness, his green eyes piercing. "And that," he said, "is precisely why I did not touch him."

"I don't understand."

"Because you love him."

"I *what*?"

He smiled. "I think you are correct," he said. "You may have possibly found a suitor."

She sat in shock, trying to comprehend what he was saying. How could he know that? How could *she* know that? She'd met Hermes De Norville twice in her life, and already her own brother was telling her that she was in love with him. It was more than insane; it was purely ludicrous. She simply couldn't love a man she didn't know.

…could she?

Bennet watched his sister's expression fluctuate in the dim light, and he smiled; she was so damnably confused that it was laughable. But there was no mistaking his observations of his sister with the knight—he'd never seen an expression of such peace on her face when the knight held her in his embrace.

Bennet had known Catrine all of her nineteen years and seen a great many emotions from her, but never one quite like that. He was jealous and suspicious and thrilled all at the same time, but he put it all aside for the moment. He would deal with the knight if, and when, he returned, and the interest was deemed truly serious. In faith, he could hardly believe that it would be, but he had not the courage to tell his sister his real opinion.

"You must clear him from your mind for a moment," he said after a pause, rising from his overstuffed chair. "We must attend vespers, and your thoughts must be pure."

She looked rather pale at the suggestion but dutifully followed her brother to the door. "What…what if he punishes me for the knight's visit?" she said, coming to a halt as he opened the oak panel. "What if he reads my mind, Bennet? What if he knows what I feel?"

Bennet shook his head. "He can't read your mind," he said. "But he can see your expression. Don't give him an advantage against you."

Catrine swallowed hard, struggling to erase any evidence of thoughts of her knight from her face. God forbid the beast should know.

She couldn't even entertain the possibility.

CHAPTER SIX

"REST EASY, LOVE."

The accent was so heavy it sounded like "looove." Hermes thought he was dreaming, or hallucinating at the very least, until a sharp pain to his eyebrow rudely jolted him. He must have flinched, because the voice cackled again.

"Ah, my brave lad, does it hurt now?" the woman asked gently, dabbing at a huge gash that sliced through his right eyebrow. "I'll stitch it up for ye, as good as new."

He tried to move, but there was pain radiating from every part of his anatomy when he did so, so he wisely decided to remain still. He opened his eyes, which seemed to be the only movement he could accomplish without suffering terrible agony. His fuzzy gaze moved over a single dim room with thatched walls and a dirt floor. There was some sort of a lamp by his head, giving off weak light, and streamers of sunlight penetrated minute gaps in the walls. A thin woman in a worn dress busied herself beside him, and he blinked, noting that she was threading a needle. When she saw that he was watching her, she smiled at him.

"Awake, are we?" she asked. She leaned over him, pinching the wound above his eyebrow together. "A few stitches, 'tis all."

He felt the prick as she started to sew. "Who are you?"

She concentrated on her work. "A mere peasant, m'lord, who thought to help ye."

"Help me?" He blinked again, thinking of his last memories, tumbling down the hill in the rain. He sighed heavily and closed his eyes, relieved that he was actually still alive. "Christ, I thought I was dead."

"Not quite," she said. "My daughter found ye this morn after the sun rose, lying in a heap at the bottom of Castle Draygon. Did ye go there to post yer bones?"

He opened his eyes, realizing what she was referring to, and feelings of darkness and dread filled him immediately. "Nay," he said, and couldn't help his voice from sounding cold. "I'm a stranger to this province. Why are there dead bodies on the wall of that place?"

The woman paused and looked at him before starting up again. Her smile was fading. "Then ye saw them," he said quietly.

"They're hard to miss. Why are they there?"

Her smile vanished completely, and she moved to re-thread her needle. It was obvious that she was uncomfortable discussing the subject.

"'Tis the curse of Draygon, m'lord," she said.

The woman went to continue with her stitches, and he grabbed her wrist, stopping her. "I've heard of this curse," he said. "It seems to be all people around here can speak of, but that does not explain why there are dead bodies on the walls of that castle. There are bones in the mortar itself. Why in the hell aren't they buried in holy ground?"

Her faded blue eyes met his with fear and trepidation. "Ye cannot understand, being a stranger to us."

He was damn tired of hearing that. "So, I'm a stranger," he said. "It doesn't mean I'm stupid. I can understand local folklore as well as the next fool."

The woman sighed faintly, resigned to an explanation she didn't want to give. Before she could speak, however, a voice rose from the shadows.

"What you saw on the walls of Draygon were the village dead," said a strong, feminine voice. "The villeins blame the curse. They post the bodies of their dead on the walls so that the souls of the dead will satisfy the fury of the bishop who enacted the curse. It is said that souls must be sacrificed until he is appeased."

Hermes and the woman tending him turned to the source of the voice. Outlined in the open door with the weak morning light flooding in at her back stood another woman. She was holding a basket filled with items, so heavy that it required both hands. She moved into the room with strong, sure feet and set the basket down beside the blazing hearth. Hermes noticed for the first time that there was an iron pot on the fire, with something boiling inside, and the woman sat down next to her basket and began to strip the leaves off plants Hermes could not immediately identify.

She was a tall woman, perhaps somewhere around her thirtieth year in age. She had long hair, the color of honey, secured at the nape of her neck, and eyes the color of storm clouds. They were haunting eyes, silver in color with a hint of blue. He'd never seen anything like them until he looked at the mother and realized she had the same silver-blue eyes. Whereas the mother was rather average in appearance, the daughter was striking: she had fine facial bones and a pert nose that wriggled as she tore up the plants. In spite of her age, he could detect no lines on her flawless skin.

He thought she was rather pretty.

"Their method of internment seems rather barbaric," he said after a moment.

The young woman nodded as the older woman continued to stitch Hermes's wound. "It is," she agreed. "But the people around here are idiots. I would expect no less."

She spoke extremely well for a peasant. Hermes watched her stir up the boiling pot. "'Twas you who found me?" he asked.

The young woman nodded. "I was out foraging for roots and stumbled across you," she said. "I thought you were just another victim of the curse until I saw you breathe and realized that you weren't dead after all. But your horse did not survive."

"I know."

"A nasty spill. He broke his neck."

He sighed, already missing the strong silver charger that had served him well. "I should be grateful that my neck wasn't broken as well."

"What were you doing at Draygon?"

He was casual in the face of her question. "Business," he said, and changed the subject. "May I have the names of the women who saved me?"

The older, thinner woman smiled. She seemed to be doing a lot of smiling at him. "I'm Hester," she said. "My daughter is Gisla."

Hermes looked strangely at the older woman, with her crude accent and appearance. The name of her daughter was spoken with melody. *Geese-la...* It was a lovely name, and very aristocratic. He wondered how a peasant woman in the wilds of Cumbria had heard of such a name.

"My thanks, Mistress Hester and daughter Gisla," he said. "When I have the strength to move, I shall retrieve my bags and pay you for your help."

Gisla rose from her position by the hearth and went to the corner of the room. Something heavy suddenly hit the floor beside Hermes's bed, and he glanced over, realizing she had thrown his saddlebags at him.

"I retrieved them for you," she said, standing over him with her hands on her hips. "You do not think I'd leave them for someone to scavenge, do you?"

She had a forceful manner. Hermes had overlooked it during the first few moments of their introduction, but now he found it wearing on him. Another few minutes with this aggressive woman and he was quickly going to be miserable. He found himself wishing he wasn't indebted to her, for he could only imagine she would never let him forget it. He'd come across women like her before, and they were all the same.

"My thanks," he said, eyeing her as he fumbled with the leather tie of one of his bags. Searching inside, he pulled out a leather pouch, weighed it in his hand, and tossed it at her. "Here. Take it."

She caught it deftly. Giving him the same expression he was giving her, sort of a dubious glare, she opened the bag. Viewing the contents, she couldn't help but gasp in awe.

"M'lord is…generous," she said, her forceful manner suddenly subdued. "There's gold coins in here, enough to buy half of England."

He waved her off and lay back on the bed as Hester covered his stitched wound with a piece of boiled linen. He fingered the clean cloth. "You put purified linen on my injury. Do you know something of the care of wounds, then?"

Hester nodded proudly. "Gisla makes an art of it. I've learned all I can from my daughter."

Hermes looked at Gisla as she counted her loot. "You know something of healing?"

She snorted. "Something, indeed."

Hester wrapped a long piece of cloth around Hermes's head to keep the boiled linen in place. "She's known throughout the fiefdom as a great healer," the old woman said. "Why, we have people from miles around coming to her for help. And with the curse that's spread across this land, that's a great many people. Ye're very fortunate she came across ye."

He almost shook his head; no wonder the woman was so strong and arrogant. She was damn full of herself, he would wager. He didn't want to mention the fact that he was a trained physic, purely because it would draw the battle lines between them. Until he could properly defend himself against an overbearing wench, it was better that she believe he knew nothing of the arts. He didn't want her to try her worth by doing vengeful experiments on him while he was weak and unable to protect himself.

"I am fortunate, indeed," he replied humbly.

Gisla didn't reply. She was back at her boiling pot. "Do you have a name, knight?"

"Sir Hermes De Norville."

"From whence do you hail?"

"Northumberland."

"And you're here on business?"

"Aye."

She didn't believe him, but to her credit, she didn't call him an outright liar. She stirred the pot a minute more or so before dipping a cup into the boiling brew. She brought it to him, hissing when the hot droplets stung her tender wrist.

"Here," she said, kneeling beside him. "Drink this."

Here came the tough part. He didn't want to appear an ungrateful patient, but he wasn't about to submit to her yet-unproven skills.

"What is it?" he asked warily.

She lacked the patience of a good physic and pursed her lips in frustration. "Don't be such a coward. Drink it up."

"Not until you tell me what it is."

She sighed irritably. "A potion of boiled willow bark and foxglove."

His eyebrows lifted; the willow bark eased minor pain, but it also made him extremely sleepy. The foxglove was better used for ailments of the heart. Too much and it could kill. He had no way of knowing how much foxglove was in the potion.

"Truly, I'm not in much pain," he said. "I don't need it."

"Don't be foolish," she snapped. "Drink it."

"I don't want it."

"Drink it!"

"Nay."

She hissed. "Why are you being so difficult? I'm trying to help you, you dimwit."

Dimwit, was it? And oh, but he would love to tell her what he knew of being "helpful." He had been helpful far longer than she had.

"You have already been invaluable to me, Mistress Gisla," he said steadily. "Please don't be insulted with my refusal. Truly, I don't believe I need a pain potion.

She cocked an eyebrow. "You're battered and bruised all over. Though your arms and legs seem intact, I would wager to say you have several broken ribs. How can you tell me that you're not in pain?"

"I didn't say I was not," he corrected. "But it is manageable. I promise that if it becomes too much, then I shall gladly drink your potion."

There wasn't much she could say in argument. He was being perfectly reasonable, and she wasn't going to force it down his throat. With a look of disgust, she poured the potion back into the pot and stirred frustratedly. He very nearly laughed at her but turned away before she could see his smile. Hester, intimidated by the confrontation between her daughter and the patient, finally re-entered the situation by putting a crude blanket on Hermes.

"Sleep, then, Sir Knight," she said. "By morn ye'll be better."

"Or dead," he mumbled.

"What was that?" Gisla asked, and stopped stirring her pot. She was sure he had just insulted her, though she could not be positive.

"Nothing," Hermes said a bit louder. Closing his eyes, he thought the very best thing for all of them at this moment would be for him to sleep. But his mind was still working, even as he tried to relax. "Mistress

Gisla?"

She was peeved at him for not answering her question. "What is it?"

"How far away is Castle Draygon from here?"

Her irritation faded. She glanced at her mother, unsure of his question. "Not far," she said. "A few miles perhaps. Why?"

His eyes suddenly opened, and he looked up at her. "Did you drag me over miles of countryside by yourself?"

She turned back to her pot. "I had an ox to carry the heavier things I was gathering. It was simply a matter of slinging you over his back."

"How on earth did you lift me?"

"Mam and I did together," she said. "We tied a rope around your wrists and hauled you up like a sack of grain, using the strength of the oxen. But why do you want to know how far we are from Draygon?"

"Because I'm going back."

The women passed glances, and Gisla finally slapped her thigh in frustration. "Then why am I making the effort to heal you?" she exclaimed. "Returning to Draygon will surely mean your death."

His gaze was steady. "It will not kill me," he said. "I don't believe in a curse and I don't believe in a dragon. Whatever manifests itself in that castle is of this earth. And if it is of this earth, then it can be battled. And battles can be won."

For the first time, all of the arrogance and defiance seemed to bleed away from Gisla's manner. She stared at him a long, long moment before shaking her head.

"Whatever is up there nearly killed you," she said quietly. "You would go back and face it?"

"What nearly killed me was a slick road and too much rain."

She was almost pleading. "So, you feel the need to defeat the legend of Castle Draygon?" she said. "Why would you do this?"

"I feel no need at all. But I made a promise I intend to keep."

"And what is that?"

"I promised the peasants of Draygon's village that I would get to the bottom of this alleged curse," he said. "I promised them that I would bring them the heads of the Dragon and his sister should the myth prove to be true."

Gisla was torn between fasciation and outrage. "You can't possibly be serious."

"Never more so."

"But *why*?"

"Because a knight never goes back on his word."

"But what stake do you have in all of this? Is the village paying you for your services as a curse-ender?"

He thought of Catrine, her lovely face and supple body. He recollected the chemistry between them, like nothing he had ever experienced. Closing his eyes, he imagined those deep green eyes smoldering at him, and it was enough to make him sweat.

"Trust me when I tell you I have a large stake in all of this," he muttered. "And I intend to fulfill my promise."

Gisla shook her head; she could see there was no reasoning with him. Knights were a peculiar breed when they spoke of the sanctity of an oath, no matter how stupid the oath happened to be.

"Then I suppose I'd better heal you quickly so you can fulfill this silly vow," she said, annoyed.

"I'll mend fast enough."

She returned to her pot. "But I found you and healed you; therefore, I am responsible for you."

"Nay, you are not. Though I do thank you for your assistance."

Glaring at him, she shook the stirring spoon in his direction. "I'm going with you to Draygon, and that's the end of it," she said. "Do you think I'm going to let anything happen to you after I struggled to save your miserable life? I've an interest to protect."

He wasn't going to argue. "Draygon is no place for you," he said.

"You would do well enough to stay here."

She frowned. "Don't tell me where my place is," she snapped. "I'm going with you, and you can't stop me. Besides, you'll need a guide. That place is a labyrinth."

"And how would you know that?"

Gisla suddenly stopped stirring. She stared into the flame of the hearth, and in the corner, Hester's gaze was fixed on the task at hand. It seemed that neither woman could look at the other. Finally, Gisla looked at Hermes with a strange expression between embarrassment and pride.

"Because I was born there," she said softly. "Trust me when I tell you that I know the place well."

The mystery grew.

CHAPTER SEVEN

ERMES WAS FINISHED playing games.

There was so much he didn't know about Castle Draygon, and Catrine and her enigmatic brother, but clearly these two women knew much, and he wanted to know what they knew.

"Then tell me everything," he half demanded, half pleaded. "What is it about this place that has everyone so fearful? That has the walls built of the dead?"

Gisla glanced at her mother, who seemed to be supportive if her daughter wished to speak more about the place. At least she wasn't shaking her head, silently begging her daughter to keep her mouth shut about the castle that was like having hell in their own backyard.

Gisla put her spoon down. "My mother used to serve the lady of the castle, long ago," she said quietly. "Her name was Lady Juliane. My father worked in the gardens."

Hermes shifted on his makeshift bed, trying to get more comfortable. "The villagers told me about the lady of the house," he said. "They said she was the most beautiful in the land and that her husband was crazed with jealousy. They told me that he killed his wife's suitors."

Gisla nodded. "Those are the bones you see in the wall," she said.

"Put there to discourage suitors for his wife's affection. But there is far more to it."

"What more?"

"If you heard the tales, then you know that one of those killed was the nephew to the king," Gisla said. "He was killed and put in the wall. When he never returned home, the king sent his favorite bishop to look for him, thinking a bishop could find out what had become of the nephew."

"Did he?"

She shrugged. "Rumor says that the bishop was murdered for prying into the nephew's disappearance," she said. "But the truth…it is much different."

"From what the villagers told me?"

Gisla nodded reluctantly. "What I tell you can go no further, my lord," she said. "If it does, we could all be in grave danger."

"I will not repeat it."

"Your oath?"

"You have it."

That seemed to ease Gisla a little. "We do not speak with the villagers," she said. "Like those who live in Draygon, we are pariahs. We do not go near Draygon's village, and they leave us in peace, but if they knew the truth…they might not leave us in peace at all."

"What is the truth?"

Gisla sighed faintly. For such a bold and brave woman, it was odd to see her fearful of a mere story. "The truth is that the visiting bishop had come for another reason," she said. "My mother was present when everything happened, so she heard and saw the truth of the situation. It's not simply that the bishop came to Draygon to discover what happened to the nephew. He came for another reason, too."

"What reason is there?

"He came for the wealth."

"What wealth?"

"Draygon is very rich, m'lord," Hester said. "Have ye not heard that story?"

"Clearly I have not," Hermes said. "This seems to be a castle with many stories."

Hester moved her stool so that she could speak to him directly. "But they all connect," she said. "Draygon used to be a fine and good castle, m'lord. For centuries, it stood strong. The lord who built Draygon was from Normandy, a pirate some say, who stole great riches and brought it to Draygon and buried it. The legend of Draygon's riches is a legend in the north, and some say that is why the bishop came. Some say that he was not a bishop at all, but a treasure hunter who lied and said he was sent by the king. He heard the rumors about Draygon's wealth and wanted to see for himself. Wealth that legend says is buried in the walls."

Hermes was beginning to understand. "So he came to hunt for the treasure," he said. "But he was killed for saying that he'd come to investigate the nephew's disappearance? To gain access to the castle?"

Hester's gaze was intense with the memories of the past, old fears that never died. "The lord told Lady Juliane that the bishop was sent to the wall," she muttered. "I heard him tell her. I heard her weep. You see, the bones are there as a warning to men who would come to seek Juliane's attention. But they served another purpose—to discourage men from tearing into the walls to look for the treasure."

The light of understanding went on in Hermes's eyes. "Ah," he said. "I see now. That is why the walls are built of bones."

Hester nodded. "Aye," she said. "The bones are a warning...for different reasons, but warnings nonetheless."

Hermes thought heavily on that situation. Considering he had been in the walls of Draygon, he supposed that he counted himself fortunate that he'd escaped alive. But he also thought on how Catrine tried to hurry him away, begging him to leave when all he wanted to do was gaze at her beauty.

She knew what happened to men who lingered too long at Draygon.

Now, it was all starting to make sense.

"But you said there is much more to this," he said. "For example, who is that man who rushes out to fight ghosts and then disappears into a wardrobe when he is finished?"

Hester knew exactly whom he meant. "Ye saw him, did ye?"

"I did."

"That is Lord Marmion," she said. "That is Juliane's father. He's quite mad but quite harmless. At least, he was the last time I saw him. He received a blow to the head in a battle many years ago and lost his mind as a result."

Hermes understood. "But what of the others who live at Draygon?" he asked. "The Dragon and his sister? *Who* are these people whom the villagers believe have cursed them?"

For the first time, Hester's expression seemed to take on some sympathy. "They are the son and daughter of Juliane and her terrible husband," she said. "They've not cursed the villagers, but something at Draygon has."

"What do you mean?"

Hester looked at Gisla, noting her daughter's pained expression, before continuing. "The son, who is the Lord of Draygon, is Bennet de la Pare," she said softly. "Gisla was born at Draygon just after Bennet was, and the two of them spent their younger years together, carefree for the most part. Bennet was sent away when he was nearly eleven years of age, but before he left, he swore he'd return to marry Gisla. They loved each other as children. That has not changed. Did ye not notice how old my girl is?"

Gisla heard her. "Mother," she said. "Do not say such things."

But Hester was unrepentant. "She's old because she'll not marry if she cannot marry Bennet," she said, almost defiantly. "Bennet's younger sister is the fair Catrine."

"The Angel of Death," Hermes muttered. "That's what the villagers called her."

Hester sighed sharply. "'Tis not true," she said. "At least, Catrine is not doing it of her own free will."

Hermes frowned. "What do you mean?"

Hester was hesitant to continue, but only for a moment. When the words came out, they were in a burst, as if they were all rushing to get out, fearful they might never get out at all. Too many things had kept those words in, for years.

But today, they were coming out. Secrets were being revealed.

"Something evil lives at Draygon," Hester said. "I saw it before I took Gisla and fled, back in the days when Bennet's father murdered Juliane and then took his own life. Bennet returned, but he was not the same boy who had left. There is something on his face…something terrible that has turned him into someone we do not recognize. It is the curse, the bishop's curse, that has turned him into a beast. But he is not the evil, Sir Knight. The evil resides in the tower, something that watches over Draygon and Bennet and Catrine and forces Catrine to its bidding."

Hermes was trying to imagine a nameless, faceless horror that loomed over Draygon, but he wasn't quite sure what she meant.

"What evil?" he said. "You mean the curse? How can it reside in the tower?"

Hester shook his head. "Ye misunderstand," she said. "I speak of something alive. A living evil, not the curse. But I'll tell ye of the curse— the bishop came for the treasure under the guise of investigating the king's nephew, but he fell in love with Juliane. As the lord prepared to murder him, the bishop spewed a curse upon the de la Pare family."

"What *kind* of a curse?"

"One of misery, of pain," Hester said. "No de la Pare family member shall live without misery and pain. If he could not have the treasure, and Juliane, then he would make the family suffer. And die away."

Hermes had heard enough. It was a complex and dark situation that seemed to grow by leaps and bounds. Bones in the walls to ward off suitors and treasure hunters, a curse from a dying bishop that the family should suffer and die away because he could not have the treasure or the lady of the castle, and an evil that lived in the tower. Any one of those things would have been enough to keep people away from the castle, but the darkness lingering over Castle Draygon ran deep.

With Catrine in the middle of it.

"I will say again that I do not believe in curses or witches or anything else magical," he said. "I am a practical man in all things, but it still doesn't explain why Catrine is called the Angel of Death."

"I go into the village more often than my mother," Gisla said. "Not too often, only to conduct business with merchants on occasion, but from what I've heard, whenever Catrine is seen in town, people start dying afterward. She comes into the village on the full moon, usually."

That didn't make much sense to Hermes. "The woman doesn't carry a curse with her," he said. "That's simply not possible. If people die after she comes into town, then it must be something else. It's not as if she can carry death with her and wish it upon them."

"I told you that I do not believe Catrine is doing it of her own free will," Hester said quietly. "The evil at Draygon—I believe it is responsible. Something is making her do it."

"Making her do *what*?"

"Something that kills."

"For what purpose?"

Hester smiled, but it was without humor. "Fear is a great motivator," she said. "Mayhap she's being threatened with being punished if she doesn't do as she's told."

"True enough. But what is the motivation for all of this?"

Hester winked at him. "And if people are dying after she comes to town, and ye know Castle Draygon is full of evil, would ye have any inclination to go near it? If ye knew only death and curses await ye?"

A flicker of realization came to Hermes's eyes. "Another way to keep treasure seekers away?"

"Possibly."

It was a great deal to absorb. There was far more happening at that dreadful castle than he could have imagined, but as he pondered what he'd been told, he had questions as well.

He looked at Gisla. "Have you had any contact with Bennet since you fled the castle?" he asked.

Gisla nodded, but the subject was clearly painful. "There was a time, once," she said. "But he will not see me. He will not see anyone. I was so young when we fled, and as I grew older, and wiser, I would sneak into the castle through the secret ways I remembered as a child. There was a time when I would go to Bennet's chamber door and talk to him through the panel, but he would never open it. He told me that I must forget about him. He told me never to return, but I did, a few times, until he simply stopped speaking to me."

"Did you ever see Catrine?"

"I did," Gisla said. "But she did not see me. This was a few years ago, and I've not been back since. If Bennet will not speak with me, there is no point in going."

"Yet you've not married."

Gisla stiffened as if it was an offensive question. "I do not need to marry," she said. "That is a falsehood that the church tells women. I do not need to marry, and I shan't."

"Not if she can't have Bennet," Hester said, watching Gisla turn away angrily. "If she will not tell ye, I will. Her heart belongs to Bennet and it always will."

Truthfully, that explained a lot about Gisla, why she was bold and brusque and abrasive. The woman loved a man she could never have, and given that Hermes had lost his wife, he understood what that was like. He'd spent years traveling around, drinking and paying for whores and being generally directionless, so he knew how a lost love could damage the human heart. Oddly, he felt somewhat of a kindred spirit to Gisla.

But none of what he heard lessened his determination to save Catrine. That was what this entire situation was boiling down to.

"I want you to listen to me and listen well," he said, though it wasn't rudely spoken. "I believe we can help one another."

Gisla's head came up. "Why?" she said. "What help could you possibly give us?"

Hermes shifted so that he could see her better from his position on the floor. "I told you that I am going to Castle Draygon to get to the bottom of this curse," he said. "But hearing the truth behind the legends and the curses tells me that there is far more happening than the villagers know. Their view of Draygon is very limited. Clearly, much more is going on."

"I've tried to tell you that."

Hermes finally sat up, wincing because of his painful ribs and head. When Hester tried to help him, he held out a hand to her to hold her off. He needed to do it himself.

He was stubborn that way.

"I am a healer," he said quietly, telling them something he hadn't planned on revealing. "I was a physic to the king's troops, having learned the healing arts from my grandfather. I know, and have always known, that any ailment a man has is rooted in something real. That means I do not believe in curses. That means that if Bennet de la Pare is afflicted with something that changes his skin, then there must be a cause of it. Something that can be healed."

Gisla was listening with morbid curiosity. "But he's had it for twenty years," she said. "Twenty years of this affliction. Even if it is not cause by curses or magic, it has become part of him."

"And you would not want to try to heal him?"

Gisla grew agitated. "How?" she said. "He will not open the door. Any visit to Draygon is taking one's life in one's hands. How can I heal a man who does not want to be healed?"

Hermes was listening carefully. "How do you know that?" he said. "Have you asked him?"

"He has made that obvious by sending me away."

Hermes considered that. "I would think any man would want to be healed if there is a chance," he said, impassioned in his plea. "But this evil in the tower… Do you think that is the cause of his affliction?"

Gisla threw up her hands helplessly. "I do not know."

"Do you know what the evil is? *Who* it is?"

Gisla and Hester looked at each other. It was Hester who finally spoke. "I suspect who it is," she said reluctantly. "But I do not know for certain."

"Who do you think it is?"

Hester was fearful even to speak her suspicions out loud. "When Lord de la Pare killed his wife, he was never seen again," she said. "Rumor said that he killed himself, too, but there was no burial because the priests whispered that there was no body. It is possible—but I do not know for certain—that he's the evil in the tower."

Hermes's eyebrows rose. "If that's true, then it would make sense as to why Bennet and Catrine never leave the castle," he said. "They're still obeying and protecting their father somehow."

Hester lifted her shoulders in a helpless gesture. "I do not know," she said. "But *someone* is in the tower. I saw the shadow of a figure when I fled twenty years ago, so I know something is there. And the wickedness that hangs on that castle has grown worse every year.

Bennet and Catrine are part of it."

Hermes leaned back against the wall, mulling over everything he'd been told. When he awoke in this dark, cloyingly warm chamber, he'd been confused. There was a part of him that had been resistant to their assistance. But the conversation about Castle Draygon and, consequently, the occupants had changed that. Something was going on at that castle, indeed, and he had no idea why he should want to even try to help. He'd spent the past few years of his life wandering aimlessly, committing to nothing, taking part in nothing. Life was passing him by.

But a pair of lovely eyes had changed that.

Now, he wanted to be part of something. To make a difference. Perhaps he was choosing a battle that might be too great to surmount, but at least he could try. A beautiful young woman needed help, and according to Gisla, so did a young man with an affliction. Two people in need of assistance.

Perhaps it was time for Hermes to reclaim his honor.

He'd been without it for a while. He'd worked hard to forget everything he'd ever achieved, a family who loved him, and the young lass he'd loved so much, once. Why he would pick this moment, and this place, to try to reclaim some of the man that he'd lost was anyone's guess. Even he really didn't know. But it had something to do with Catrine and that horrific castle. And then it occurred to him.

He couldn't save the woman he'd lost those years ago. He'd been helpless in the situation.

But he wasn't helpless now. Perhaps he could save one for the one he lost.

He had a plan.

"Do you know of Castle Canaan?" he asked.

Both Hester and Gisla nodded. "It is not far from here," Hester said. "To the west, less than a day's ride. I remember because, long ago, the Lord of Draygon was allied with Canaan. Why do ye ask?"

Hermes shifted, his hand against his tender ribs. "Because Castle Canaan belongs to my family," he said. "If we are to solve this mystery, we are going to need help."

"What help?" Gisla asked.

Hermes fixed on her. "An army," he said. "No evil can withstand a de Wolfe army."

Gisla's eyes widened. "You will bring troops to Draygon?"

"Can you think of something better?"

Gisla blinked as if startled by the question. Then she shook her head. "Nay," she said. "But if there is a curse, are you not afraid it will be cast over the army?"

Hermes smirked, as if it was a ridiculous question he had all the answers to.

"Let them try," he muttered. "If the evil that hovers over Draygon thinks it can curse the army from Castle Canaan, I believe my cousin will have something to say about that."

"What do you mean?"

Hermes lowered himself back to the ground, more comfortable on his back. "Draygon thinks it has a curse?" he said wearily. "Then de Wolfe has the cure. The fangs of a wolf are always more frightening than the mumblings of a witch."

He seemed confident, and Gisla didn't argue with him. He closed his eyes, wounded and weary, but she sat there, watching him. Was it possible he was correct? *Were* the fangs of de Wolfe greater than the evil that infected Draygon?

She had a feeling that she was going to find out.

CHAPTER EIGHT

CATRINE HEARD THE bell before sunrise.

That was how he usually summoned her, with an old church bell that had been brought all the way from London, from a church that had burned and what remained of it shoveled into the Thames. Rumor had it that the church had been controlled by a priest dedicated to the dark arts, and God had burned it to the ground. True or not, the bell had made it out relatively unscathed.

The bell meant to summon worshippers now summoned servants of the damned.

Catrine was one of those servants. The sound of the bell woke her, and she very nearly startled herself right out of bed because she knew the Creature in the tower was demanding her presence. It was the morning she'd spoken of attempting her mission again, the Angel of Death proceeding one more time to the village to deliver the contents of a phial that would poison the villagers. Some would die, usually the very old and very young, some would only become sick, but some would feel nothing at all.

Such were the reactions to the ingredients.

Dressing quickly in a simple broadcloth dress and shoes that were badly in need of repair, she made her way to the tower. The weather had clouded over this morning, a heavy mist covering the land. The same mist smothered Castle Draygon as Catrine took the last of the tower steps and knocked on the splintering oak door.

Spindly, ancient fingers pulled it open on creaking hinges.

"It is time," he rasped. Then he extended a leather pouch that was heavy with what felt like sand. "Into the well, Catrine, and then hurry back. They may be watching for you now, so you must be careful."

With a heavy sigh, Catrine took the pouch. She knew exactly what it was, the same ingredient she always put into the water source of the village. The great irony was that she had to gather it, too. *Hemlock and foxgloves.* There were other things, too, that she couldn't even begin to guess. The Creature in the tower would prepare the ingredients himself, but he would not go outside into the sunlight, so she was forced to do his bidding and gather the things he requested.

If she didn't, the curse would only grow worse.

"I will be careful," she said, turning for the door because she hated being in the tower chamber any longer than necessary. But she paused for a brief moment. "And Bennet...he seems to be in more discomfort than usual. Will you help him today?"

Beady, dark eyes gazed steadily at her. "I will need tallow," he said. "It is the only thing causing the curse from spreading."

"But that seems to cause even worse—"

"Silence," he hissed. "Go, girl. Do as you're told. Make amends for your failure to me."

Catrine hurried from the door, nearly tripping on the top step once she was out of the chamber. She caught herself, thankfully, because it would have been a long tumble to the bottom. Sometimes, she entertained the thought of casting the Creature in the tower down those treacherous steps, and she would have already done so had she not been afraid that the curse would only grow worse.

He who was in the tower controlled the curse.

He controlled everything.

Taking the steps swiftly, Catrine made her way down to the ground level. The fog was still there, still heavy, and it was very dark. She made her way into the keep where the fire was burning low in the entry hearth and lit a fat-soaked torch from the embers. Though she did not want to be seen on her journey into the village, the truth was that she had nothing to light her way. Not even the moon. She needed something to see.

"I heard the bell."

The voice came from behind, and, startled, Catrine turned to see Bennet coming off the cylindrical stairs. He was cloaked in the darkness, anything to cover the curse that spread over him. Even in the dark, even in front of his sister, it was something he always kept hidden.

"I know," she said hurriedly. "I have just come from him. I must go to the village."

"To the well?"

"Aye."

There was a pause. "The last time you ventured there, you were nearly captured," he said. "Don't you think they will be watching for you?"

She set the torch in a bracket and reached for a tattered old cloak that hung by the entry. Pulling it across her slender shoulders, she fastened the ties at the neck.

"It will be dark because of the mist," she said. "That will aid me. I need only slip to the well and then lose myself in the trees. Even if someone is watching, I can lose myself in the trees."

Bennet drew in a long, slow breath. "Mayhap I should help you."

Catrine looked at him in shock. "Of course you will not," she said. "Imagine if they captured the Dragon of Draygon. They would kill you and take great joy in it. I could not bear it, Ben. You must stay here, as you always do. I will do what needs to be done."

She heard him sigh again, and then he moved toward her, stepping into the light of the torch she'd lit. Catrine could see the angry red bumps and pustules across his face, mostly covered by the beard he kept because it was too painful to shave it off, yet the hair aggravated his condition, so he had to suffer with it. It was particularly bad today. At the moment, he had a huge lump on the right side of his jaw. She could see it. It would go down, with time, then reappear somewhere else on his face.

Such was the way of the curse.

"I wish it was not this way for us," he said. "I have been thinking of our earlier conversation when we spoke of the knight who had come to help. I should not have been so cruel about it, Cate. That was the bitter side of me speaking."

Catrine knew that. Bennet wasn't evil by nature, but the years of rejection and despair had infected him as much as the curse had. It was part of his very composition now, traits that came out in brutal and snappish ways at times.

"You needn't worry," she said. "I know you, brother. I know you do not mean half the things you say."

He grunted regretfully, knowing she spoke the truth. "I wish this was something we did not have to face together," he said quietly. "You want a family, and that should be your right. But not me. I can endure this curse because I must. I pay for the sins of our father. But you… Sometimes I wonder what he would do were you to run away. I wonder if he would use his black magic to find you and force you to return or if he would simply let you go."

Catrine shook her head. "He needs me too much," she said. "He needs me to do his bidding as you cannot. But truthfully… I would not leave you to face this alone, Ben. It is not the curse I fear as much as it is leaving you behind to endure what God or Lucifer or whomever would force us to endure. We are paying the penitence for those sins of the past. The burden is ours to bear, brother. Together."

There was great pain in Bennet's eyes, something Catrine couldn't stand to see, so she pulled the hood over her head, grasped her cloak, and fled out into the early morning.

Out to do what she was forced to do.

The Angel of Death was on the prowl.

CHAPTER NINE

H E COULD HEAR the distant roar.

Somehow, it was morning and Hermes was awake, lifting his head to the sounds of a roar. He didn't even remember falling asleep the night before, right after he'd given his missive for Castle Canaan to a local farmer's son whom Gisla had supplied. The boy took a shilling, possibly more money than he'd ever seen in his life, and had fled on his surefooted pony as the moonbeams bathed the countryside in a ghostly light and distant clouds began to appear in the west. The boy was off, Hermes fell into a deep sleep, and now he'd awoken with a distinct sense of foreboding.

"What is that noise?" he asked sleepily, grunting when his angry ribs caused him pain.

Gisla was already up, already at the window of the cottage that faced the valley where Castle Draygon was situated. She was in a sleeping shift, a heavy shawl pulled around her shoulders, as she unlatched the shutters that covered the window.

"I am not certain," she said, trying to see through the fog. "The mist has come, but the sounds are coming from the village."

"How can you tell?"

"Because the villagers are a noisy bunch," she said. "I've heard this manner of discord before. We are on the rise of the hill and sounds carry up the slope, even more with the mist. Something is happening."

Hermes slowly sat up, his hand on his ribcage. "At this hour of the morning?"

"At any hour of the morning," Gisla said, coming away from the window and moving quickly toward the chamber where she had been sleeping. "Hurry; don your clothing. We must see what is transpiring."

Hermes frowned. "Why?" he asked. "Why should we be concerned with disgruntled villagers?"

Gisla paused at the door. "Because the only thing they are usually disgruntled about comes from that castle," she said. "If Castle Draygon is of any concern to you, you will get dressed."

With that, she bolted into the chamber and shut the door. Hermes could hear her speaking to Hester, and that sense of foreboding he'd awoken with began to intensify.

Something was happening in the village.

He could only hope it wasn't what he thought it was.

Grabbing for his clothing, he prepared himself for the worst.

CHAPTER TEN

S HE HADN'T MEANT to hurt her.

Catrine had made it to the well in the darkness and in the mist, ditching her torch in the trees surrounding the village before making her way toward the well. Luckily, she knew the area well, so she was able to get her bearings, even in the mist, but the sun was clearly beginning to rise because the mist was lightening. She knew she hadn't much time before the women of the village were awake and gathering water for their daily chores.

She had to hurry.

The village well wasn't a large well, but it was one that kept a plentiful supply of water. It never ran dry. In fact, the ground around it was constantly muddy because of the groundwater that seeped from the well, so the entire area had the smell of mildew. Mixed with the foliage and compost, it made for a pungent scent.

Catrine lingered at the edge of the trees as lights began to appear in the windows of the cottages, and she knew the time to complete her task was now, before she was seen. Before everyone in the village awoke and knew what she was up to. That was how she'd been captured the last time.

She had to act.

Slipping from the trees, Catrine quickly moved across the mud that smelled of mildew, being careful not to slip, as she approached the well. It was surrounded by stone with a winch and a bucket, and a big trough where people gathered their water. Further down the trough, the water dumped into a stone pond of sorts where women did their wash. Opening up the pouch, she dumped the contents straight into the well.

Catrine paused for a moment, watching the ingredients sink into the dark water before turning away. She planned to rush back into the trees, covering her tracks, but the moment she turned around, she ran straight into an old woman with an earthenware container for water in her arms.

Startled, Catrine panicked. She was moving too quickly to stop and ended up plowing into the old woman. The earthenware container went flying and the woman fell backward, right onto the ground. She hit her head on a rock, one of many on the rocky ground, and the blood began to flow. As the woman lay there and wailed, Catrine bolted for the safety of the trees.

But the damage was done.

People were up, doors flying open at the sound of the wailing. The old woman was crying *engel, engle*, which was the old term for angel. It sounded like *in-gull*, now shouted all over the village. Villagers began to take up the cry—the Angel of Death had been sighted again. People began to emerge from their cottages with clubs and any other weapon they could get their hands on.

Catrine knew she was dead if they caught her.

Fortunately, the trees provided some protection. It was still early enough, and people were still confused enough, that no one was running after her at the moment, but she knew that would quickly change. She began to run like the wind, panic fueling her unnatural speed as she darted through the trees and out onto the road that lead to

Castle Draygon.

Soon, she knew the road would be full of villagers heading for Draygon. They usually stayed away from the castle, but after they'd captured her so recently, she suspected their bravery would be fed, especially if they thought they could catch her again. They wouldn't go beyond the walls of the castle, or at least they never had, but she wasn't entirely sure that would be the case this time.

They might come after her in earnest.

It seemed as if she ran for hours. In the mist, and with the angle of the valley, she could hear the dull buzz from the village and people continuing to cry out that the Angel of Death had visited them. It was faint, but unmistakable. Catrine continued to run, losing her shoe at one point, but she didn't stop. She kept running, chewing up the flesh of her foot on the sharp, rocky soil.

She had to make it back to the castle.

But her energy was beginning to wane. The villagers had horses, and she knew they could easily catch up to her if she didn't push herself, so she pushed until she could hardly breathe. She felt like vomiting. Her breath began to come in panicked gasps; she was convinced that she might not make it home before she was overtaken by the angry villagers. Villagers who now had a poisoned water supply, poison intended to keep them away from Draygon. To perpetuate the legend of the curse.

But she suspected it was only inciting them to rebellion now.

The road was becoming more familiar now, and she knew she was coming close to the castle. Wiping the water from her eyes, she began to see the hulking, bone-filled walls outlined in the mist. The sun was rising, the sky was turning white and gray, and those horrible bones were increasingly apparent. Bones of men who had come to call on her mother or bones of men who were caught in the wrong place at the wrong time. So many tales behind those horrific bones.

So much death and despair.

As the gatehouse of Draygon came into view, someone grabbed Catrine's arm.

She screamed and lost her footing. She would have pitched to the ground had the strong hand not stopped her. Then there were two hands on her.

Catrine found herself looking into Hermes's concerned face.

"What's happening?" he asked, his face pinched red from the cold. "We heard the alarm in the village. What happened?"

Catrine couldn't tell him. She tried to pull away, but he wouldn't let her. She finally screamed at him.

"They will kill us all!" she said. "Release me!"

"I will not release you," Hermes said calmly. "Tell me what happened. Why are they shouting the alarm?"

Catrine was starting to feel faint. "Please," she begged, tears running down her cheeks. "Please let me go. I must get to safety or they will kill me. They'll kill us all!"

A woman appeared next to Hermes, her gaze riveted to Catrine. "She's right," the woman said. "We cannot stand out here. We must get to safety."

Catrine recognized the woman. Years ago, she'd worked at Castle Draygon. So many years ago. Catrine had seen her since, but it was years since they'd last met. Her panic was now peppered with confusion.

"Gisla?" she said, incredulous. "Is that you?"

Gisla reached out to take one of Catrine's arms. "Come," she said to both Catrine and Hermes. "We must go inside. There is no time to waste."

Hermes followed because Gisla's manner seemed urgent. In fact, it had been Gisla who demanded they head straight for the castle when the roar of the village roused them. There had never been any talk of going to the village itself, but only to the castle. Everything pointed toward those bony walls and towering keep. They had only just arrived a few moments ago when they saw Catrine running up the steep and muddy road.

Now, Hermes had his broadsword out, taking both horses in hand as he followed the women into the small outer bailey and then to the vast and derelict inner bailey. Odd how he didn't even notice the bones this time around. They were part of the walls, part of this vast and horrific place, but he wasn't looking at them. He was focused on other things. The sun was rising more now, burning off the mist, as he searched for a place to hide the horses as Gisla led Catrine toward the keep.

"Wait," he called out to them before they could reach the stairs that led to the entry. "Let me find a safe place for the horses before you go in."

Gisla pointed to a broken fence, a cluttered corral, and a large stone building that was missing half the roof.

"In there," she said, gesturing toward the structure. "Put them in there. Hurry!"

Hermes could hear the strain in her tone and quickly moved the animals into what had once been a stable. There were no bones in the walls here, simply crumbling stone. He found a couple of stalls that weren't damaged, so he put the horses in there, both of them stout ponies belonging to Gisla, and grabbed his saddlebags. He never went anywhere without them. Sword still in hand, he rushed off toward the keep.

When Gisla saw him coming, she pulled Catrine up the stairs, running for the entry. Hermes, sore ribs and all, closed in quickly behind them. He was moving swiftly but not without pain. However, he ignored it. He had since he'd awoken to the dull roar in Gisla's cottage. They'd rushed to Castle Draygon because Gisla insisted.

No painful ribs were going to stop him from coming. Especially if Catrine was involved.

The interior of the keep was dark, just as it was the first time he'd been there. Catrine and Gisla were trying to throw the old, heavy iron bolts, but Hermes stepped in and used his considerable strength to secure them. Once the door was bolted, he turned to Catrine in the darkness.

"Now," he said with strained patience. "Tell me what happened. Why were you running up the road?"

Catrine's eyes glimmered in the dim light, and he could see tears forming. "I…I had to," she whispered. "Please do not be angry with me. You saved me from such a fate when we first met, but I had to return. You must understand that."

He frowned. "I will understand if you tell me why," he said. "What are you doing?"

She blinked and tears coursed down her cheeks. "Please do not ask," she said. "You must simply trust that it is something I must do."

"*What* must you do?"

Catrine simply hung her head, wiping at the tears on her face. But Hermes remembered what Hester had told him—*something evil lives at Draygon and forces Catrine to do its bidding.* He remembered those words clearly and could see how much his questions distressed Catrine. He'd told the villagers that he would get to the bottom of what happened at Castle Draygon, and here he was.

Now, he wanted to get to the bottom of it more than ever.

For Catrine's sake.

"Catrine," he said, his voice considerably softer. "I know of the rumors. I know about the treasure and the curse. I know why there are bones in the walls. I know all of that. I also know that there is something evil here, something that curses your brother and forces you to do its bidding. Won't you tell me where, and what, this evil is? I swear to you that all I want to do is help."

Catrine's head snapped up and she looked at him in shock. "You…you must not speak those words," she whispered. "Do not speak of it. Do not say it!"

Hermes reached out and grasped her, his grip strong. "Tell me," he said quietly but firmly. "I can help you. But you must tell me what it is. Or do you enjoy living in fear?"

His words wounded her, but they also made her think. She didn't know how to reply. She was already edgy enough, and now Hermes was forcing her to confront everything she didn't want to confront. Her nervous gaze moved to Gisla, who was looking at her with great concern, but she saw no help in the woman's eyes. No hint of how she should respond. Slowly, her focus returned to Hermes.

This strong, handsome knight had returned. Truthfully, she could hardly believe it, but here he was. To her, that meant the things he said yesterday had meaning. He meant what he'd said. He'd returned and was concerned with what was going on. He wanted to help. She'd never known anyone who wanted to help her, not in her entire life, so the concept was alien.

But help had arrived, in the flesh.

She simply didn't know how to take it.

"It is the way of things," she finally said. "It must be this way."

"Why?"

"If you know the rumor as you say you do, then you already know the answer."

"If I knew the answer, I would not be asking," he said, growing frustrated. "I have come to assist you. I have summoned others to help also. I can change your life, Catrine. Don't you understand that?"

"She does."

The voice came from the cylindrical stairs, deep and raspy. Gisla gasped, startled by the voice, but Hermes didn't show any reaction other than to look in the direction of the stairs. He could see a great, hulking figure on the steps, lingering in the shadows. He still had his broadsword, so he was armed. He didn't feel threatened, at least not at the moment.

He studied the shadow.

"Are you the evil?" he finally asked. "Or are you Bennet?"

"It's Bennet," Gisla whispered tightly. "I would know his voice anywhere."

The figure seemed to shift, movement in the dark as he turned in her direction. The voice that came forth was incredulous. "Gisla?"

"It is I."

They heard the figure exhale, long and slow. "It has been a long time," he said after several moments, emotion in his tone. "What are you doing here?"

Gisla was struggling not to burst into tears at the sight, or at least at the shadow, of the only man she'd ever loved. She hadn't really expected to see him, although given that he lived here, she didn't know what she *had* expected. It had been so very long. In any case, his appearance had her off guard and deeply emotional. As if all of the pent-up longing and anguish of being separated from him had suddenly found a crack in the walls she tried so hard to keep intact. Walls of self-preservation, built by broken dreams.

After all these years, it was a wall that was more fragile than she had realized.

"We could hear the chaos in the village," she said, her voice trembling. "Somehow…somehow I knew that Catrine was involved. This knight has sworn to… He was injured yesterday after leaving Draygon, and I tended him. He told me what happened yesterday with Catrine, and he swore to the villagers that he would get to the bottom of what is happening at Draygon, so when we heard the trouble, I brought him here. He says he means to help, and I believe him."

The figure shifted again. "Your voice is like music to my ears," he murmured. But just as quickly, his voice turned hard. "And you, knight. Why should you be concerned with Draygon? I spared you once when you came here to see my sister, but I cannot promise I shall continue to show mercy. Your intrusion is not welcome."

Hermes believed him without question. There was hazard in the man's tone, this Dragon of Draygon, but Hermes didn't back down. Those angelic eyes of the man's sister were looking at him with such fear that it enraged him.

What was going on at this place that had everyone so bitter and terrified?

"I can see that," he said steadily. "I can see that there is no gratitude in your sister's face or in your voice, no gratitude that a stranger might actually mean what he says. No appreciation that a stranger with honor has arrived at your doorstep with the intent to help you. Do you see how you live, man? Do you see these crumbling walls? Do you see your sister living in filth and fear, a lovely young woman who should be dressed in the finest silks with a husband who adores her, yet she remains here, and you let her. Why on earth would you be satisfied with the life around you? Why would you *not* want any help?"

The air was so still and silent after that little speech that Hermes could hear Catrine's rapid breathing next to him. That was the only thing he could hear until the figure on the stairs moved slightly.

"You do not understand," he said in a low and less angry voice. "We are not your concern."

"Then you like living as you do?"

"This is our home."

"That does not make it some glorious shrine to the decrepit life you lead," Hermes said. "It only makes it a hell you choose to immerse yourself in. That does not make you noble, my lord. It makes you weak."

"Insult me again and I will do what I have done with so many others."

"Nay, Ben," Catrine said anxiously. "You promised."

But Hermes held out a hand to her, stopping her. His focus was on Bennet. "You may try," he said. "But know that I am a knight of the highest order, trained by the House of de Wolfe, the House of de Norville, and the House of de Winter. If you still feel that you can fight me and win, then I encourage you to try. But know it will not be a simple thing."

The air was full of apprehension now. It was fairly crackling with it. The figure took one step, and then another, moving down the flight of stairs slowly. The implication was clear. Both Catrine and Gisla went out to meet him, putting themselves between two big men to prevent any physical confrontation.

"Nay," Gisla said. "Ben, please… Let their be no fighting. He truly only wishes to help, and in that sense, he is not wrong. If there is a chance that you should be happy in life, would you not want to take it? I…I brought him here because I wish that for you. I have always wished that for you."

Bennet had come to the bottom of the stairs. He was still in the shadows, but the light from the dawning day was beginning to stream in through the lancet windows, lightening the entry. It was clear that Bennet was clad in a cloak of some kind that covered his entire body and most of his face. The only thing evident was his left eye and part of his right, but the hood of the cloak was covering everything else.

Those bright eyes were looking at Gisla.

"He does not understand," he said to her. "While the offer of help is admirable, there is nothing he can do, and I will not be insulted in my own home."

"But how do you know I cannot do anything?" Hermes said. Then he threw out his hand, indicating the chamber around him. "Your sister deserves better than this. Gisla thinks well of you. I know that she was once in love with you and you with her, but this place has come between you. This *curse* has come between you. What is this evil in the tower that claims this place and bends you both to its will? Is it a demon?"

"We do not speak of it."

"Then you permit it to control you."

"I would say that, once again, you do not understand."

"Then explain it to me. I am not stupid."

"It is none of your affair."

That was the truth. Hermes knew that, but he couldn't accept it. He couldn't accept this hulk of a man, covered from head to toe, who refused to fight back against the life that had claimed him.

Defeat.

That was what Hermes sensed more than anything. Pure, bitter defeat. Even if the brother was defeated, the sister still had some life in her.

Hermes turned to Catrine. "Come away with me," he said, going to her. "You do not have to remain here. Come with me, away from this place, and I will show you a more glorious life than you can imagine."

Catrine was torn between refusal and great interest. "You cannot be serious," she said, sounding both hopeful and fearful. "But we have only just met. How can you ask me such a thing?"

Hermes could see the resistance in her eyes, but it was thinly held. "I don't know how," he said. "Only that it feels right. It *must* be right. Come with me and we shall be married."

Before she could answer, something heavy crashed against the entry door. Both Catrine and Gisla shrieked, startled and frightened, as Hermes raced to the small arrow slit overlooking the inner bailey.

All he could see were torches and pitchforks.

"The villagers," he said. "They're in the bailey."

With a cry, Catrine raced to another arrow slit with Gisla on her heels. They strained to see what Hermes was seeing.

They could see the flaming torches, too.

"They've come for me." Catrine gasped in terror. "They've come to kill us all!"

"They cannot get inside," Hermes said, looking at the heavily fortified keep door. "Unless there is another door down below where they can enter, this door should hold."

"There is no other way to enter the keep," Bennet said, though he made no move to go to the windows like the others were. "They could burn that door down and it would still hold because of the iron reinforcement. There is no way they can enter."

Hermes simply nodded, but he was still concerned. He had a broadsword and an assortment of daggers, but he suspected that was it for weapons in the keep. He looked at Bennet.

"Do you have a sword?" he asked. "On the slight chance they should somehow enter, what do you have to defend yourself with?"

"*Aux aremes!*"

The shout came not from Bennet, but from the enormous wardrobe next to the cylindrical stairs. Abruptly, the doors flew open and the little man with the sword began his fight again for a new day. He began swinging the weapon around madly, narrowly missing Hermes, who stepped out of the way to avoid being sliced. The old man was hissing and hollering as he did battle with unseen foes again.

"*Tu es un lache!*" he said. "*Tu dois mourir!*"

The battle with the phantoms quickly grew intense. Hermes remained by the lancet window, alternately watching the crowd below and the old man as both of them rose to a fight. The old man, however, didn't seem overly concerned with the live bodies standing around him. He was only concerned with those that no one else could see but him, thrusting and slicing and, at one point, falling down because an unseen opponent had knocked him to his knees.

That was when the drama increased.

Now, they were apparently fist-fighting on the ground. The grunting and kicking and rolling around on the floor was curious, but Hermes's attention moved to the villagers as they tried to find something to batter the door down with. He was concerned that they would find the horses in the stable and try to steal them, but so far, they remained away from the old stone stable. They were more concerned with the outer bailey.

They began to bring rocks into the inner ward, heading for the keep. Big, solid boulders of granite. As Hermes watched with interest, they threw them against the door, rattling it but not breaking it. There weren't even any cracks. When they realized that, they went looking for something else to use against the door.

The minutes began to pass.

Minutes began to stretch out. One became two, and two became four. Five, ten, fifteen minutes passed slowly and laboriously. The old man from the wardrobe eventually returned to his lair, bruised and battered from fighting ghostly opponents, while Hermes remained by the window, watching the villagers as they made a kindle pile next to the door, clearly attempting to burn it down. Given that the stairs were also wooden, he wondered if they realized their stairs would burn as well.

Oddly enough, he wasn't as concerned as he had been. He was fairly certain the villagers wouldn't be able to accomplish what they'd set out to do, so his attention began to return to Catrine, who was still standing with Gisla, watching the happenings in the bailey below. Seeing the woman for the third time since he first met her only solidified the feeling of familiarity he had with her. The hair, the face, everything about her had seemed familiar from the onset, and he knew why. He hadn't wanted to admit it to himself for reasons he didn't fully understand, but he realized that Catrine was the woman from his dream.

Help me, Hermes!

That dream he'd had more than once. Though the face of the woman in his dream was obscured, or not exactly clear, as if he was looking at her underwater, the shape of the eyes and the color of the hair were Catrine's. He'd always thought the dream to be remnants of his wife's passing, something his mind had concocted because he lived in constant guilt that he'd been unable to save her. In fact, that was what his grandfather had told him, too. *It is simply your imagination, Hermes,* Paris had said. *It is trying to rationalize your inability to help your wife.*

He'd believed his grandfather for the most part.

But now, he wasn't so sure.

He'd started out determined to get to the bottom of the evil at Castle Draygon. It was something he'd promised the villagers. But that focus had shifted to Catrine and the life she led. It shifted to the way she made him feel, the sense of determination that he had to help her.

Help me, Hermes!

That was where all of his do-good ambition had come from.

She was the lady from his dream.

But he didn't know if she'd believe that. He wasn't even really sure *he* did, but the coincidence was too great to ignore. But the brother… Hermes found himself looking in the direction of the figure of Bennet de la Pare. Gisla had remained by the window with Catrine, watching the villagers, as Bennet lurked near the great staircase that led to the upper floors. He hadn't come out of the shadows. This man, this "dragon," who was so cursed that Gisla had been sent away, never to love anyone else.

That was coming to be part of the mystery.

Hermes came away from the window. Slowly, he moved in Bennet's direction. Throughout this entire assault by the villagers, the man had not shown one ounce of concern. He'd remained in the shadows, protecting his identity, clearly untroubled that people were trying to break down his door. Even now, he had his back against the wall, his head lowered, and he hadn't moved from that position in quite some time. Hermes didn't want to startle the man for fear that he'd lash out, so he stopped when he was within several feet of Bennet.

He studied that lowered head before speaking.

"My name is Hermes de Norville," he said quietly and steadily. "I've been rude not to introduce myself before this moment. But I want you to understand that I truly mean you no harm. I was raised by men who were compassionate and brave, and if they saw a situation that needed assistance, they were inclined to give it. I once asked my grandfather why he was intent on doing good things, and he told me that he hoped it would balance out his life with God. He'd killed many men in battle and hoped that by doing good to those in need, and by living a decent life when he could, he would be weighed and measured fairly when his time came."

Bennet stirred. "Is that why you are here?" he asked, his voice raspy. "To right yourself in the eyes of God?"

"I am here because I am a man of reason and intelligence," Hermes said. "I am also a man of skill. I have been taught the healing arts by my grandfather, Paris de Norville. He taught me all that he knew. I understand you have an affliction. Will you tell me what it is? Mayhap I can help."

He asked kindly, in a way that Bennet couldn't take offense to. There was genuine concern in the tone. But Bennet shook his head.

"No one can help," he said. "It is my burden to bear and no one can help."

"Has anyone tried?"

"There is no point."

"How do you know unless you try?" Hermes said, truly not trying to be aggressive in his questions. "It is possible that I can help you. Is it an illness? Are you in pain?"

Bennet shifted on his big legs. "It is a curse."

"I do not believe in curses or magic."

"That is your privilege."

At least Bennet was being calm about it, which wasn't usual with him. Somehow, Hermes sensed that, and he didn't want the conversation to turn sour. If he helped the brother, perhaps it would pave the way for his good intentions toward Catrine.

All he knew was that he wasn't leaving Draygon without her.

"I've heard that men call you the Dragon," he said after a moment. "Is it because of this affliction?"

Bennet shifted again, perhaps a bit restlessly. "Among other things."

"But why the Dragon?" Hermes asked. "Do you breathe fire? Or are there horns beneath that cloak?"

"No horns."

Bennet wasn't chasing Hermes away, but he wasn't being receptive, either. "I have brought my medicaments with me," Hermes said, hoping that might garner some interest. "If you will only show me your hand, I can see what the affliction is. Mayhap it is something that is curable."

"It is not."

"Will you at least let me try?" Hermes said, pressing gently. "If I fail, you will be no worse off than you were before. Are you not tired of living with it? Would it not be more desirable to have some relief if such a thing is possible?"

Bennet sighed heavily. After a moment, he lifted his head slightly and Hermes could see his eyes. "You do not understand," Bennet said. "This curse…it is my penitence for the sins of my father. I am meant to bear it. God does not want me to feel relief. He wants me to feel torment."

"May I at least see your hand?"

Bennet grunted. Then a hand suddenly shot out from underneath his cloak. "There," he said. "Look and be done with it. Once you have seen it, do not ask again."

Hermes took his actions seriously. The light from the morning was the only thing illuminating the entry, meaning that the light was very poor for inspecting Bennet's hand. But he quickly went to the man, trying to get a look at what had been referred to as the curse. He could see red, scaly skin but couldn't get a good look at it, so he gestured to the lancet window that overlooked the bailey.

"Will you let me see it in the light?" he said. "I cannot see it well here."

Bennet's gaze flicked to Gisla, over at the other window.

"Nay," he said, retracting his hand. "That is not necessary."

Hermes immediately realized what had him so self-conscious. He didn't want Gisla to see him in the light. Perhaps they'd loved each other for years, and perhaps he saw that love as something that had stagnated and would never blossom, but he still didn't want the woman he'd once loved deeply to see the depths of his affliction.

That gave Hermes an idea.

The hearth was next to Bennet, and Hermes quickly moved to the wood box, only to see very little wood in the bottom of it. Scraps, really, and old scraps at that. He picked one up and hunted for a flint and stone somewhere around the hearth, only to find the flint on the stone mantel. Using the hearthstone, he struck the flint and lit one of the scraps of kindling. A small blaze erupted from the end, and he held it up to Bennet.

"I will keep my back turned to the ladies so they will not see any-thing," he said quietly. "Let me see your hand again."

Bennet eyed him warily. "There is no need."

"Please."

Bennet almost denied him again but gave up after a moment. Perhaps part of him wanted Hermes to look at it. No one had for many years, and the only help he received was from the Creature in the tower, who sent down tallow he'd infused with mysterious ingredients. But the tallow never seemed to help, even if it did give some initial relief to the dryness of the affliction. After a while, however, the tallow seemed to make it worse. Bennet had accepted that until this very moment.

Perhaps he really didn't like suffering. Perhaps here, there was a real chance.

Slowly, he extended his hand again.

Hermes bent over the appendage, inspecting it closely without touching it. He had Bennet turn his hand over several times, showing the red, scaly skin and angry, bleeding patches. Hermes was able to coax him into lifting the sleeve a little so he could see Bennet's arms, and he was faced with more dry, scaly skin, but he was also faced with angry red bumps and pustules just above the elbow. That was as far as Bennet would lift his cloak, but for Hermes, it was enough.

He looked the man in the eye. "Let me see your face," he said quietly.

A flicker of uncertainty flashed in Bennet's eyes, and he looked over to the women, still gathered by the window. As long as they weren't looking at him, he was braver. He kept the hood of the cloak pinned over his face so that only his eyes were showing. Hesitantly, he removed the pin, and the hood fell open.

A bearded face greeted Hermes, but he could see that beneath the beard was a sea of blistering red pustules. They went all over the man's face, cheeks, chin, neck, and forehead. They were everywhere, distorting his features. Without asking permission, Hermes reached up and lifted the beard slightly, trying to get a good look at what lay beneath. When Gisla said something to Catrine over by the window,

Bennet quickly pinned up his hood again so only his eyes were visible.

Standing back, Hermes pondered what he'd just seen. It was horrific, to be certain, but he'd seen it before. Not so severe, but he'd seen it before. In fact, one of his grandfather's knights had a lesser version of what he thought Bennet had.

"Do you have any vinegar?" Hermes asked.

Bennet looked confused. "Vinegar?" he said. "Why?"

Hermes gestured to the man's neck and chest. "Do you have the pustules on your neck and chest and back?"

Bennet nodded. "Aye."

"Everywhere?"

"Mostly."

"And the painful scales on the skin? Is that merely on your hands and arms?"

Bennet snorted. "That is why I am called the Dragon," he said. "Those scales appeared when I was a young man. Others saw it and the rumors spread. Dragons have scales and so do I."

It made perfect sense to Hermes, superstitious idiots spreading their superstitious lies. But what Hermes saw wasn't a curse or magic. He thought Bennet ought to know.

"What you have is not a curse," he said quietly. "I do not know who has told you that, but it is not a curse. I have seen it before. I can tell you how to help it, but you must stop using the tallow. That is only making it worse."

Bennet's expression turned incredulous. "But I have had this since I was a young man," he insisted. "I was fostering when it came upon me, and my master sent me home, hearing of my family's curse. He did not want me near his home or family."

Hermes lifted an eyebrow. "I am going to be honest with you," he said. "Whoever has told you it is a curse is wrong. They are using it to convince you that you are cursed, but I am telling you that you are not.

I may not be able to cure the affliction, but I can tell you how to help it."

Bennet was astonished. "Are you certain of this?"

"I can only try. Are you willing?"

"What must I do?"

"The vinegar," Hermes said. "Soak rags in it and apply it to the bumps. Everywhere there are bumps, lay the cloths on the area. Do this every day, three times a day. But for the dry and painful skin that looks like scales, I will make you a potion to apply. It should help."

Bennet was listening intently. "But not the vinegar?"

Hermes shook his head. "Not to that," he said. "You have two different afflictions that require two different treatments. I will do what I can."

Bennet was trying very hard not to look hopeful, but he was. It was the most hope he'd had since his affliction started. He'd become immune to the idea that the curse was somehow curable, convinced it was God's will, but the strange knight thought otherwise. Bennet didn't want to give Hermes's suggestions any credit.

But he couldn't help himself.

"And you believe it will make a difference?" he finally asked.

"I believe it may help."

Bennet opened his mouth to reply, but movement caught his eye. Looking over Hermes's head, he could see Gisla standing several feet away. His gaze met hers, and, for a moment, they simply stared at one another. Bennet wondered how much she'd heard, if any. They were separated because of this curse he held. Had she heard the same words of hope that he had? Was it possible their dismal future without one another might actually change?

But Gisla gave no indication that she'd heard. She was mostly looking at Hermes when she spoke softly.

"They are trying to burn the door down now," she said. "They sent some men back to the village to obtain oil."

Bennet covered up his hands, making sure his face was properly concealed, because he didn't want Gisla to see any of his flesh.

"They will only succeed in burning the stairs," he said, pushing past both Hermes and Gisla. "I thought they would grow tired of this, but I can see that I was wrong. I will send them away for good."

He went straight to the entry door. Catrine was still by the window, gasping with fear when her brother threw the big bolts, releasing the last vestiges of protection between them and the villagers. Before she could stop him, Bennet threw the door open, much to the shock of the startled villagers, and tossed back his cloak.

His curse, in all its glory, was revealed.

"Go before I curse you all!" he boomed in a terrifying voice. "Any man remaining shall suffer my wrath and shall post his bones upon my wall as a warning to all men who would threaten the Dragon of Draygon. My patience is at an end. Leave now or suffer your doom!"

The villagers gazed upon the bumpy, scaly, enormous man with the electrifying voice and fled for their lives. They scurried down the stairs, some of them falling and getting trampled by others. They were moving so quickly that they simply weren't watching where they were going, nor did they care. They headed for the outer bailey and the gatehouse beyond as Bennet came down the stairs, shouting and bellowing, chasing them out of his castle. When he was satisfied that he'd sufficiently terrorized them, he pulled the cloak back over his shoulders and pulled the hood over his head, closing it as he turned for the keep.

His work was done.

Gisla and Hermes were standing in the open door, watching the remains of the villagers flee. Bennet didn't look at either of them as he took the stairs quickly and disappeared inside. Gisla ducked in after him, but Hermes lingered on the stairs, making sure the villagers were truly gone, before following the others inside and shutting the door, bolting it.

It had been an impressive exhibition.

No wonder the man hadn't been concerned with villagers at his door if he had that kind of power. Hermes was going to tell him so, but Bennet was already rushing up that enormous staircase, disappearing into the floor above.

"Where is he going?" Hermes asked.

Gisla simply shook her head and turned away, but Catrine answered. "Back to his chamber," she said. "What you saw… That has happened before. It is rare the villagers come here, but it has happened before. Bennet told me once that he feels like an animal when he chases them away like that. He uses his affliction to scare them off. There is no dignity to frightening people with your appearance."

Hermes could hear the sorrow in her voice. "I saw his skin," he told her. "I believe I can help him, but I will need your assistance."

Catrine looked anxious. "But how is that possible? God has given him that curse. It is punishment for my father's sins!"

Hermes shook his head. "God may have given him the affliction, but it is not a curse," he said firmly. "It is no more a curse than the color of your hair or the color of your eyes. It is simply God's will, but it can be helped. Will you help me?"

Catrine was fascinated. "But what can I do?"

Hermes smiled to let her know that he was confident in the help he could give. "Vinegar," he said. "I need all you can find, and I will need rags. Will you do this?"

Catrine was hesitant, but she glanced at Gisla only to see the woman nodding at her. "Do as he says," Gisla said. "I think I know what he wants to do. Shall I go with you?"

Catrine wasn't oblivious to who Gisla was or what she had once meant to Bennet. Truthfully, Catrine remembered everything, though the memory of Gisla had faded. But here she was, as large as life, and old feelings and memories were starting to stir again. Even Catrine could see that.

And she wasn't disappointed.

"Aye," she said. "If it will help Bennet, I should like to have your assistance."

Gisla smiled and took Catrine by the hand. Together, they disappeared into a corridor off the main entry, leaving Hermes alone in that terrible, cavernous entryway that smelled of rot. But that didn't matter.

He had a job to do, one that could possibly gain him a wife.

And perhaps even end a man's torment.

He went to work.

CHAPTER ELEVEN

B Y THE TIME Hermes had everything he needed, the day was beginning to wane.

The villagers hadn't returned, which was a good sign, but the old and creaking castle was beginning to close in around him. Lord Marmion had made another appearance toward midday, fighting phantoms on the staircase this time. He even appeared to "die" on the stairs, because he lay there for some time before picking himself up and retreating into a wardrobe that reeked heavily of human habitation. He may have been a harmless old man, but he was living in filth.

Filth that covered Draygon itself.

But Hermes couldn't concern himself with a madman. He had spent his time in a chamber off the main entry, one that was derelict and dusty, but it had a table, and that was what he needed. He'd brought his saddlebags and laid them upon the table, opening up both of them. Since he always carried his medicaments with him, it was just a matter of finding what he was looking for. He intended to make a salve for the dry, itchy skin that infested Bennet's hands and lower arms, and he was able to pull together what ingredients he needed, but only in small quantities. If this salve worked, he could make more of it, in larger quantities, but he had to start somewhere.

He started with honey.

Honey had miraculous healing properties, he'd been taught, and indeed, it could be used on many skin conditions. So did the calendula flower, and he had a small pouch of the petals, which he mashed into some wild honey that he had, beeswax, and a little bit of water. He'd collected the honeycomb to use for sweetening, because he had a sweet tooth, but it had crystalized. Now, he was crushing it up with the calendula leaves, and soon he would heat it so the honey melted again, creating a salve of sorts.

He'd seen it work before on skin ailments.

He also sent the women to fetch oats, which were usually plentiful in the north and used for animal fodder or for a peasant's meal. He was convinced that he could help Bennet even though the man seemed to be entrenched in the idea that his skin issues were a curse. Hermes had heard the rumors, and now, he'd seen the Dragon of Draygon in person.

But he wasn't a dragon. He was a man.

That was where the superstitious villagers had gotten it wrong. They were a foolish lot and considered Bennet some kind of demon. Perhaps because of the way he behaved, they had no other alternative. But Hermes knew better. Bennet wasn't a demon, but a man with problems. Yet, for all of the rational explanations Hermes could find, there was one outstanding.

The evil in the tower.

It was a subject heavy on his mind when Catrine and Gisla joined him in the small chamber, arms full of the things he'd sent for. The vinegar was really only wine that had turned sour, but it would do. Catrine fully admitted to drinking the sour wine because they had nothing else, but Hermes assured her that he would pay for what he used, even if it was for Bennet's benefit.

But he vowed that Catrine would never drink sour wine again.

He kept Catrine with him while Gisla went back for the oats. He put Catrine on pouring the soured wine into a bowl they'd managed to find, and as she poured, he pretended to busy himself.

But he was really keeping his eye on her.

"I was prepared to buy the oats myself," he told her. "I thought you might not have any."

"There is a local farmer willing to give us oats in trade for things of value we might have," she said. "He knew my grandfather and remembers him as a good man. He is not afraid of us like the villagers are."

Hermes paused. "Catrine, may I ask you a question?"

"I think so."

"Without you becoming hysterical?"

"What question would it be?"

He looked at her. "Who is in the tower?" he said. "We are quite alone. I promise you are safe. Will you please tell me who is in the tower?"

She met his gaze. Her first reaction was to refuse to answer and run away, but she realized how much work he was willing to do for Bennet. No one had ever been willing to help, not ever, and certainly no one had showed them such kindness. Hermes may have been a pushy stranger, but he was a stranger who was going to help them whether or not they wanted it. He saw something they did not, a hope they had long forgotten or perhaps never even had, but now they felt it, too. It was contagious.

Torn, but perhaps resigned, she sat on the nearest stool that wasn't a broken-down mess.

"I do not know his name," she finally murmured.

"Then it is a man?" Hermes asked.

She nodded. "Aye," she said, barely above a whisper. "A man. An evil man."

"But who is he?"

She sighed heavily and looked at her hands. "He came because of my mother's legendary beauty," she said. "The king's nephew had—"

He cut her off when he thought he understood what she was telling him. "Then it's the bishop," he hissed. "Is that who is up in the tower?"

She looked at him, shaking her head. "Nay," she said. "The bishop came seeking the truth about the king's nephew, whom he thought had been murdered by my father. But he wasn't killed at all."

"Then if not the bishop, who is in the tower?"

"The king's nephew."

Hermes's eyebrows rose. "Henry's *nephew* is the evil in the tower?"

She nodded, a flicker of pain crossing her face. "He came for my mother's beauty, but local legend told him of the treasure buried deep in Draygon," she said. "He is the one who created the curse, who spread the rumors, who posted the bones on the walls to keep others away. He is the one who makes me go to the village every full moon and put his poison into the well."

Hermes was shocked. "He has done all of this?" he said, aghast. "But why poison the water?"

"To keep up the appearance of the curse," she said, tears beginning to fill her eyes. "He is waiting for Bennet to die, I know it. He is waiting for my brother to die so he can have the castle all to himself and find the treasure."

She was beginning to get upset, and Hermes went to her, putting his hands on her arms in a comforting gesture. "Then he doesn't know where the treasure is?"

Catrine sniffled. "Nay," she said. "Bennet will not tell him, so he has brought this curse around him. He tells Bennet that as soon as he is told the location of the treasure, he will lift the curse, but Bennet will not tell him and the curse remains. Now, he is waiting for my brother to die of his affliction."

She was beginning to cry. Hermes pulled her against him, his big arms going about her, as she sobbed against him. Truthfully, he was astonished by what he was hearing.

"But your brother said he is suffering the curse of his father," he said. "He said he was paying for his father's sins."

She sniffled again. "It is true that my father would kill or maim those who came to seek my mother's beauty," she said. "Why wouldn't he? He was her husband. But my mother succumbed to the king's nephew's charms and then killed herself when my father discovered the tryst. When my father confronted the king's nephew, he pushed my father down the stairs. The fall killed him. I was so young at the time, and Bennet was still fostering, but the king's nephew wasted no time in spreading rumors and sending word to Berkeley Castle, where Bennet was, to tell my brother's master that the entire de la Pare family was cursed. They sent Bennet home after that."

Hermes held her tightly as he processed what she had told him. He'd been told a different version of the shocking story, but this one seemed to make much more sense to him.

Greed, treasure, and lust. All of them a catalyst for man's darker nature.

"So a greedy man seduces the wife, kills the husband, and two small children become his prisoners," he finally mumbled as the scenario began to make perfect sense. "He controls the children by telling you that the House of de la Pare is cursed. Bennet has been stricken with a skin condition that I have seen before, and the man uses that as proof of the curse."

"Aye."

"And you?"

She shrugged, giving in to Hermes's warmth and affection, things she had been starved for her entire life. "I do his bidding," she said, feeling ashamed and fearful and confused. "I have always done his bidding."

"By poisoning the well?"

"And other things."

"What other things?"

She lifted her head to look at him. "I make sure we eat," she said. "I sell what I can or trade services for food."

He cocked an eyebrow because he didn't like the sound of that. "*What* services, Catrine?"

"Labor," she said. "For the farmer I purchase the oats from, sometimes I do chores at his farm to pay for the grain."

He was relieved to hear that her services didn't mean something lascivious or degrading, but it was still beneath her to labor like a common servant. "I see," he said. "And this has been going on for many years."

She nodded wearily. "Many, many years."

Hermes sighed faintly as he mulled everything over again. He pulled Catrine against him in a tight embrace just because he liked it. Somehow, feeling her softness and warmth against his body helped him think more clearly. The feel of a woman could do astonishing things to a man's state of mind.

"Why hasn't Bennet chased him away?" he asked after a moment. "He's a big man. He's strong. Surely he can take care of an old man in a tower?"

Catrine let him pull her closer, her body caving in to his as if she had no bones at all. As good as she felt to him, he felt equally good to her.

"Because my brother's spirit is broken," she said. "The affliction of his skin has ruined his entire life. He loved Gisla but refused to marry her because he could not bear to have her touch his skin, knowing how repugnant it must be to her. He has let the evil convince him that he is cursed and that is something he deserves. It is difficult to explain how someone as strong and intelligent as my brother can be beaten down by rumors and witchcraft, but when your spirit is broken, you are willing to accept most anything."

"It sounds to me as if he has simply given up."

"He has."

Hermes held her for a few more moments before gently releasing her and looking her in the eye.

"If something is broken, it can be fixed," he said. "I believe I can help your brother, but not for the altruistic purposes I have implied. I'm doing it for you."

"Why for me?"

"Because if I do something good for him, mayhap he will agree to a marriage."

It was a little manipulative, but not in a terrible way. Bennet would know relief and perhaps—just *perhaps*—they could have that normal life they'd often spoken of. Away from the curse, away from the horrors of Draygon. An idea that was so fragile it regularly slipped away until, as the years passed, it became less and less important. Like the dream it was these days. But with the appearance of Hermes, suddenly, the dream was more tangible than ever before.

But it wasn't as if she was any great prize.

"Why?" she managed to ask. "What is it about me that you find so alluring? Is it my rich clothing or expensive perfume?"

She was jesting in a sense, trying to find a reason, but that wasn't something he could easily give. However, in the spirit of honesty, he told her the truth.

God's honest truth.

"Because I have dreamt of you," he said, averting his gaze because it sounded silly as he spoke it aloud. "I've had a recurring dream since my wife died a few years ago. In the dream, a woman is hanging from a cliff and is begging me to save her. My grandfather told me that I have the dream because I was unable to save my wife, so I am tormented by that failure. I always thought that was the reason for the dream, too, until I saw you. Your voice… Your hair… It is like the woman in my dreams. I believe I have been brought here for a reason, Catrine. I believe you and your brother need my help. Give me a chance to save you. Give me a chance to prove I'm not a failure. I cannot explain it to you better than that."

She was looking at him seriously. "I'm very sorry to hear about your wife," she said. "May I ask what happened?"

"Childbirth."

She sighed. "That is very sad, indeed," she said. "But it was not your fault."

That was obvious, yet it was something Hermes wrestled with. He had since it happened. Unwilling to delve into a tragedy that had transformed him into the traveling, drinking, whoring man that he'd become since that time, he found it easier to focus on Catrine and her immediate problem. Perhaps, with time, he'd speak more on his wife when the time was right.

But that time wasn't now.

"It was a long time ago," he said, shifting the focus. "Where is your brother's chamber?"

Catrine pointed to the floor above. "At the top of the stairs," she said. "Why?"

Hermes went to gather the potion he'd been working on. "Because I am going to go to him and help him with the vinegar," he said. "I want you to find Gisla and take some of the oats and a little water and make a paste. Bring that paste up to me. Understood?"

Catrine nodded. "Aye."

"Good lass."

He collected the bowl he'd been working with, the one he'd used to crush the mixture in, and headed for the door. But he stopped just short of leaving the chamber, turned on his heel, and headed back to Catrine. As she watched him curiously, he slanted his lips over hers and kissed her sweetly.

With a smile to her shocked expression, he quit the chamber in earnest.

CHAPTER TWELVE

BENNET HEARD THE knock on the door.

"Who comes?" he said.

"Hermes."

Bennet grunted. He though he'd run away from the man, but it was clear that Hermes didn't give up easily. He'd found Bennet. With some frustration and perhaps even a little curiosity, he went to the door and opened it.

"What do you want?"

He wasn't wearing his cloak. His red, bumpy skin was for all to see, or at least for Hermes to see. But Hermes wasn't really looking at him; he simply pushed past Bennet and entered the chamber without being invited.

"I need to warm this mixture," he said, looking around. "Do you have a lamp? Or mayhap start a small fire in the hearth?"

Bennet was still standing by the door, shutting it when he realized Hermes had come to stay. "I don't often use either," he said. "But there is some wood in the box. Not much, but a little."

Hermes went straight to the hearth, which was taller than he was, and he was a fairly tall man. It was elaborately carved stone, covered in layers of dust and soot. In fact, it took him a moment to note the grand scale of the dusty room in general. It looked like a room a king might have occupied decades before, but with age and neglect, it was a sad shadow of its former self. Silk window coverings hung in tatters, and mice made nests in the fine furnishings. Hermes collected a piece of wood from a fine box with faded painting on the exterior. Striking a piece of flint against the stone, he lit the wood and held it beneath the pewter bowl that contained his honey and herbs.

"What is that?" Bennet asked suspiciously. "What are you doing?"

"Heating a salve," Hermes said, watching the honey melt before the bowl grew too hot for him to hold. "Now that the women are not in the chamber, will you show me the rest of your affliction?"

Bennet was standing back by the bed. "You've seen enough," he said. "The rest of me is covered with the same. It is nothing different."

The honey had finally melted enough, and Hermes tossed the flaming piece of wood into the hearth before standing up.

"Please," he said. "Remove your tunic and let me take a good look. I'll need to see where the salve his most needed."

Agreeing to the request the second time around was easier for Bennet. He didn't put up a fight as he pulled the tunic over his head, gingerly because his skin was so tender, and what Hermes was faced with was something truly painful and angry-looking. As he had suspected, Bennet's torso, neck, and shoulders were covered with red bumps, many of them full of pus, some of them burst, but he also had scaly skin that was mostly on his lower arms and hands.

Hermes inspected it all carefully.

"You have had this for a long time," he commented.

"You knew that. I told you."

Hermes was looking at the man's back before coming around front. "I know," he said. "But I can see the old scars. What else have you done for this other than the tallow you mentioned?"

Bennet was embarrassed. That much was clear. "I do not know why you should even bother asking," he muttered. "In fact, I do not know why I should even let you look at me at all."

Hermes ignored the mumbling. "Have you done anything else for this?" he repeated.

Bennet sighed sharply. "Just the tallow."

Hermes shook his head. "No more," he said. "As I told you before, that can only make it worse."

"Then what is in that bowl you put before the flame?"

Hermes opened his mouth to reply when there was a knock at the door, interrupting them. Panicked, Bennet grabbed his tunic and darted off to hide. It was such a massive chamber that he simply slipped into the shadows and was gone. Hermes waited until he was out of sight before going to the door.

Catrine and Gisla were at the door, bearing bowls and rags. Hermes could see that the oats and the vinegar had arrived, so he ushered the women into the chamber and had them set everything on a table that was leaning dangerously.

"Can we help?" Gisla asked anxiously.

Hermes was starting to see that a good deal of Bennet's reclusiveness was due to his appearance. It wasn't that the man was a hermit, or antisocial, but he had a desire to stay away from people because of how they reacted to his condition. When engaged in conversation, he was intelligent and well-spoken, so his instinct to run from people was a learned behavior. He knew how people reacted when they saw him.

And the last person he wanted to see that was Gisla.

"Not at the moment," he said. "I can manage myself, but what I cannot manage is my empty stomach. I cannot remember when I've last eaten, so it would be best if you were to prepare something for us to eat. Will you do this?"

Gisla nodded, but she still wasn't entirely eager to leave the chamber. Catrine, however, knew how her brother could be. She knew his moods. Her gaze upon Hermes was one of concern.

"Are you certain?" she asked softly. "I can stay and help if you wish."

Hermes smiled faintly at her. "I would wish for you to be near me in any case," he said, "but I am hungry. It would please me if you brought some food."

Catrine returned his smile, timidly, and urged Gisla to leave the chamber with her. When they were gone and the door shut, Hermes went to the table where they'd set down the bowls and the rags.

"They are gone," he said loudly. "You can come out now."

He could hear the shuffling as Bennet came out of the darkness and into the light. He meandered in the direction of the table, looking at the contents with interest.

"You must think I'm a fool for hiding every time someone comes near," he said. "Even my sister. Even…Gisla."

Hermes was in the process of soaking the rags in the vinegar, which was red and had dregs in it. "I do not think you foolish," he said. "You have been conditioned to do this, to hide from people. It has become your nature."

Bennet didn't reply because nothing Hermes said was untrue. He paced around behind the man, looking at the things on the table. "What is that?" he asked.

Hermes began to wring out the rags. "Vinegar," he said. "Remove your clothing and lie upon the bed."

Bennet looked at him dubiously. "All of my clothing?"

"Everywhere you have your affliction."

Bennet cocked an eyebrow. "It is on my arse."

"Then remove your breeches and lie on the bed."

Still eyeing Hermes warily, Bennet did as he was told. Hermes's confidence in his knowledge and actions had conveyed enough trust to

Bennet that he was willing to give the man a little faith. He removed his clothing and lay upon the bed, using the linen to cover his modesty, but he was nude as he had been asked. Hermes came over with the vinegar rags in his hands and began laying them carefully on the terrible red bumps on Bennet's chest.

"Christ," Bennet hissed. "That's cold. And it stings."

"I know," Hermes said. "But this will help."

Bennet flinched when Hermes put a rag on his neck. "What is the other stuff in the bowl?" he asked. "The white paste?"

"Oats and water," Hermes said. "Once you have soaked in vinegar, I am going to cover you in the oats. The honey mixture you saw me heating up will go on your hands and feet, wherever there are scales."

"And you believe this will cure me?"

"I believe it will help you."

Bennet watched Hermes as he worked, the serious manner in which he focused on his task. He'd been so opposed to Hermes at the start, but somehow, he'd let the man in, just a little. That wasn't usual with him.

He never let anyone in. Not even Gisla.

"I do not understand why you are so determined to help me," he finally said. "I'm a complete stranger. Why are you so persistent?"

Hermes glanced up at him. "Why not?" he said. "You've gone your entire life with men condemning you and with that bastard in the tower controlling you. You've forgotten that the kindness of men still exists."

Bennet's focus lingered on Hermes for a moment. "Mayhap," he said. "But in my experience, men are usually kind only when they want something."

Hermes *did* want something, but he wasn't sure that now was the time for such honesty. "I do want something," he said. "I want to feel useful again. I want to feel as if I am making a difference again. It has been too long since I have felt that way, so do not think my actions are entirely altruistic. I am here for a reason, my lord. Make no mistake. I *do* want something."

"What else could you possibly want?"

Hermes went back to the table and collected more soaked rags. "I was married a few years ago," he said, coming back to the bed. "My wife was from a good family in the north. Being both de Wolfe and de Norville gives me more of a pedigree than most men, so I had several choices when it came time to marry. Her name was Mabel, and every time I looked at her, I felt as if I could hardly breathe. It was a glorious feeling, something every man should experience at least once in his lifetime. Mabel and I were married and we were happy. I was quite happy until she died shortly after the birth of our twins."

Bennet grunted softly. "Then I am sorry for you," he said. "I cannot imagine such torment."

"Aye, you can," Hermes said as he laid the rags on Bennet's shoulders. "You have Gisla, yet you have not married her. She has never married because it seems that you are the only man she has ever loved. At least, her mother said so. If you love her in return, then you must know torment, indeed. A woman you love, just out of your reach."

It was the first time the dynamic between Bennet and Gisla had been brought up. Bennet was staring at the ceiling as Hermes continued to place the vinegar-soaked rags on him, but he didn't seem keen on responding. Hermes simply went about his business, placing the rags on all of the red, painful bumps he could find before switching over to the honey potion. As he started to smear that on Bennet's hands and wrists, Bennet spoke softly.

"I'd made myself forget about her," he said. Then he snorted unhappily. "I should not even be speaking of this. It is not your business. You do not care."

"Untrue," Hermes said. "Gisla tended to me when my horse tumbled down the side of your hill. My ribs are sore, still, and my head aches, but she saved me from death, I am certain. That means I owe her a debt, and you seem to be the only thing that truly matters to her. According to her mother, of course. She's never told me anything directly."

Bennet sighed softly. "Old Hester?"

"The same."

"She never could keep her mouth shut."

"She means well, I believe."

Bennet didn't dispute that. He remembered his mother's old lady's maid quite well. But he remembered Gisla more. Women he'd pushed from his mind, and with Gisla in particular, the more the memories of her returned to him, the more unsteady he felt. Unsteady emotionally, spiritually… The memory of a lost love could do that to a man.

"We were so young," he said. "I've known Gisla since we were both quite young."

"And you've loved her since the beginning?"

Bennet thought on the question. "Probably," he said. "In fact…in fact, I cannot remember when I have not loved her."

"You love her even now?"

"It would seem so."

Hermes looked at him. "Then why push her away?" he said. "She told me that you have pushed her away."

Bennet frowned. "Look at me," he said. "Look at where I live, the life I exist in. I could not condemn her to that."

Hermes smeared the honey potion on Bennet's left hand. "She lives in a cottage near Draygon with her mother," he said. "She has never left you. She has stayed by your side all these years, and I think you must have known that. Haven't you?"

Bennet wouldn't look at him. "I am not certain," he said. "I've not seen her in years. I've not left the castle in years. I'd hoped she had married well and moved away."

"Did you truly? Or are you lying to me?"

Bennet turned his head even further away. "Possibly both," he muttered. "Possibly neither. I think I am lying to myself more than anything."

Hermes stopped what he was doing. "If I can help your condition, it will change your world," he said with some passion. "I lost the woman I love, Bennet. The woman you love is within the walls of this castle. You do not have to lose her if you do not want to. Mayhap I am doing all of this for Gisla because I owe her a debt. If I can help you, then in turn, that might help her."

Bennet didn't seen annoyed that Hermes had used his given name. In fact, it made the situation more personal.

"Then you do this for her?" he asked.

"I think so," Hermes said quietly.

"But what about that story you told me about your grandfather being kind to others because it righted things with God?"

"That, too."

Bennet stared at him for a few moments before speaking. "It just occurred to me," he said. "It has been a long time since I've had a conversation with another man. A long time, indeed. I'd forgotten… Well, I'd simply forgotten that such a thing could be pleasant."

Hermes grinned. "As I plaster you with vinegar, you think this pleasant?"

Bennet grinned back. "Strangely, it is."

Hermes chuckled. It was the first genuinely warm moment they'd shared, all of it as he doused the man in potions and smelly liquids. Hermes finished with the honey paste on both of Bennet's hands and moved to his feet.

"If you must know the truth, it is the same for me," he said. "This is the first real conversation I've had with someone in ages. Honestly, I cannot even remember. I've spent the years since Mabel's death wandering. I simply couldn't bear to be home, in the north, where she died. Where every time I look at my children, they remind me of her. Then I met a woman whom I thought would replace Mabel in my heart and in my bed, but she fell in love with another man. I cannot blame her. I live the life of a wanderer, and I had nothing to offer her. But it was painful, nonetheless. I wander from town to town, drinking and pondering life. Conversations like this are few and far between. So is the feeling of usefulness."

Bennet was watching him. "Then it makes sense why you are so determined to help me," he said. "It gives you a feeling of worth you've not had."

Hermes glanced at him. "You are perceptive when you want to be."

Bennet smiled thinly. "I am only perceptive to others," he said. "Never with myself."

Hermes paused in his duties. "You are a big, strong knight," he said. "If you trained at Berkeley Castle, as I've been told, then you must be skilled as well. Why do you let that man in the tower control you?"

Bennet's warm expression faded. "You are wrong."

"About what?"

"I am not a knight."

Hermes's brow furrowed. "But you trained at Berkeley."

"I was sent home before I could finish my training."

That made some sense to Hermes. "I see," he said. "But that still does not answer my question. You learned something at Berkeley. You are not a weak man by any means. Why do you allow the man in the tower to control you?"

Bennet snorted wearily. "What else is there for me?" he said. "Look around, Sir Hermes—look at how and where I live. What else is there for me?"

Hermes eyed him seriously. "You've lived so many years of your life believing there is nothing left for you that you're convinced of it," he said. "You've let that fool in the tower convince you that you're cursed and worthless. But I am telling you that it is not true. I am told the bastard in the tower is here for the treasure that is supposedly buried in the walls of Draygon. I'm sure you know that. He is wants what you have."

"He'll never get his hands on it."

"But he is destroying your legacy." The last few words were spoken passionately, and Hermes immediately dropped his head, returning to his duties. "Forgive me. It is not my place to say such things, but you are clearly an intelligent man. You have a woman who loves you. I should think you would want to fight for what is your right."

Bennet was trying not to look too guilty, too defiant. "Do you know who is in the tower?" he asked.

"I know it is the king's nephew."

"My sister told you?"

"Aye."

Bennet's focus lingered on Hermes for a few moments before he turned away. "Christ," he muttered. "You must think me a horribly weak man."

Hermes finished putting the salve on Bennet's left foot. "I think you are a defeated man," he said. "I think you have resigned yourself to this miserable existence and you do not care if you live or die. It is not your fault. But it is your fault if you allow it to continue beyond this moment."

"Why this moment?"

"Because I am offering to help you," Hermes said. "If you want to escape this, then you have my sword. I will do all I can."

Bennet sat up, his dark eyes intense. "I do not understand any of this," he said. "Why should you want to help me? You give me pretty speeches about your grandfather's reasons for kindness or the fact that you want to feel useful, but how am I to know that is the truth? I simply do not know why you, a stranger, should want to help me. It seems to me that there is more to this than you are telling me."

Hermes looked at him. *Really* looked at him. If ever there was a time for honesty, it was now. If he waited and then asked for Catrine's hand at a later time, Bennet would realize that all of this kindness was meant to pave the way for Hermes's true intentions.

But it wasn't as if Bennet was totally oblivious. Hermes had stated his intentions once before. It was time to be obvious about it.

"Do you remember me telling you that a man should experience the inability to breathe in a woman's presence at least once in his lifetime?" he said.

Bennet nodded. "I do."

"That's the way I feel when I look at your sister," Hermes said. "You ask me why I want to help you? It is true that I want to help you to repay a debt to Gisla. That has not changed. It is true that I am finally feeling useful for the first time in years. I have been honest about that. And earlier today, when I came with Gisla and the villagers were pounding at the door, do you recall I asked your sister to come with me and she would not? I came yesterday, too, and asked the same thing. I wanted to take her away. I still want to take her away, but I do not want to do it without your permission. I want you to understand what kind of man I am and give your permission freely. And that is what I want, Bennet. I want a chance at happiness again with Catrine."

It was an impassioned speech, one not missed by Bennet. He understood Hermes completely and, truth be told, wasn't entirely shocked to hear what Hermes wanted. It wasn't as if the man had made a secret of it. Maybe Bennet understood him, just a little, because he was remembering what it was like to long for a woman.

"I've killed men for less," he muttered. "Like my father, I've killed men who have come to Draygon for treasure or because they saw my sister and followed her home. For any reason, really. Those bones you see in the walls—some were put there by my father, some were put there by me. I have followed my father's legacy, and on my body, I bear the curse of his sins. But you…you have been different."

Hermes eyed him. "How?"

Bennet considered the question. "Because you saved my sister from the villagers," he said. "And also because I saw how my sister looked at you when you came to Draygon the first time. I saw the interest and attraction in her face. I've never seen that before."

"And that is why you did not try to kill me?"

Bennet nodded slowly. "I could not do that to her," he said. "She has had enough pain in her life."

"Then you will permit me to marry her?"

Bennet sighed faintly, emotions rippling across his face. "You will take her away from her and give her a happy life?"

"I will do my very best to make her happy."

"You will always be good to her?"

"I swear it."

Bennet nodded. "She deserves not to live in squalor for the rest of her life," he said. "I can shoulder the burden, but she will not leave me. If you want her to come with you…then you must convince her."

Hermes was feeling a great deal of hope. "If I can help your affliction, then she will not feel as if she must stay," he said. "If I can help you, there is Gisla… I meant what I said. It is torment to love a woman and not be able to have her. And it is torment for a woman to love a man who has sent her away."

Bennet knew what he meant. "I know," he said quietly. "Let us see if your methods will help before we speak of anything further. But there is something else."

"What else?"

"The evil in the tower," Bennet said. "He will not let her go."

Hermes's eyes narrowed. "We'll see about that."

Bennet believed him.

CHAPTER THIRTEEN

THE FOOD, WHAT there was of it, was ready.

Catrine and Gisla had prepared porridge for supper with some of the bread Catrine had baked earlier in the day. It wasn't much, but it was all they had, so they made big bowls of it and prepared to take it to Hermes and Bennet.

But there was one more person Catrine would take it to.

The evil in the tower.

Leaving Gisla in the dismal, dirty kitchens to finish preparing the meager meal, Catrine headed for the tower. She walked the halls of her ancestral home with a bowl of porridge and a cup of the foul wine they'd made, heading toward the tower that looked out over the countryside. It was the place where her father had met his death, pushed down the stairs by the evil that resided in the tower. Catrine was reminded of that every time she mounted the stairs.

She was obedient so she would not suffer the same fate.

As she headed up the stairs that led to the upper floors, Lord Marmion emerged from the wardrobe again. Catrine had seen him so often that she never gave him a second thought, her grandfather whom she'd long grown immune to. She couldn't remember when he was sane.

Even as a small child, he'd hidden in the wardrobe, appearing at odd hours to attack unseen enemies. Her mother had told her that he'd been hit on the head in battle and it had changed him completely. He never left the battle he'd been injured in and fought it nightly. It was a sad legacy for a once-great knight.

But it was simply part of the curse of Draygon. A home for the mad and the tormented.

As Catrine made her way to the doorway that led to the tower stairs, she could hear Lord Marmion's fight fading, and thoughts of him faded also as Hermes began to fill her mind. In the past day, her life had changed so drastically that it was difficult to fathom. Before Hermes had saved her from the angry villagers, her life had been one of hopelessness and fear. But since his arrival, the situation had changed so much that she was still struggling to believe it was all real. Hermes, a man who had been a stranger yesterday but was a stranger no more, was determined to help Bennet and take her away from the strife of Draygon. He'd never hidden his intentions, had rather been quite honest with everything he did. She didn't know why she should trust him, or even believe him, but there was something in his manner that conveyed trustworthiness. She *wanted* to believe. And the part of her that longed for a husband and family was willing to go on a little bit of faith.

Faith had always been difficult to come by in her world.

And then there was Bennet.

For a man who had killed more than one man who had come to Draygon over the years, he'd refrained from hurting Hermes. As she'd once said, the bowels of Draygon were lined with the unfortunate living who became the fortunate dead. That was quite true. But Hermes was different, and Bennet had explained why. It was the way she looked at him, he'd said. Bennet had seen something in Catrine's expression that stilled his murderous impulses.

That expression had been one of hope.

It was the recurring theme since Hermes's arrival. Catrine had never experienced hope in her life. Her entire world had been ruled by disappointment, so the introduction of a knight willing to wrest them from their hell was truly a rarity. Even now, as she made her way up the narrow, winding tower stairs, Catrine was going to give tribute to the very person who had caused that heavy fog of hopelessness. The one who had put them in the predicament they were in today.

The one who controlled every move she made.

"Well?" a voice above rasped. "Did you deliver the ingredients?"

Catrine paused, looking up the narrow stairwell and seeing the figure above. "I did."

"I saw the villagers," he said. "I saw them coming. What has become of them?"

"They've gone away."

"Why?"

"Because Bennet chased them away."

"Good." If a tone could imply a smile, then the tone used implied a beaming one. "One would have thought they would have learned by now."

"What will they learn?"

"That if they challenge Draygon, the Dragon will roar."

Catrine continued up the stairwell, slowly. "They have gone now," she said, hoping to leave the porridge and run away. "I've brought you some nourishment."

The figure was lingering at the top of the stairs, right in front of the door leading to his chamber. "I saw someone else come, too."

Catrine came to a halt again, unable to look at him. "Aye."

"Who has come?"

Catrine wasn't sure how much she should tell him because anything she said would be twisted and used against her. "The knight who saved me from the villagers," she said. "He…he helped me again."

"Ah," the figure said. "The knight who succumbed to your charms, the one who makes your blood boil."

Catrine resumed the steps, moving quickly so she could leave the porridge and get away. "He is speaking to Bennet," she said. "I do not know what they are speaking about."

She'd reached the top, and he reached out to grasp her wrist, almost dumping the food in her hands. "Don't *you* know?" he said. "Of course he has come for a reason. Of course he has saved you from the villagers and has been kind to you. Don't you know, lass?"

Catrine was trying not to drop the bowl. "He was kind," she said. "He does not seem like the others who have come before."

Dirty nails dug into her tender flesh. "He is just like the others," he said, his thin voice brittle. "He has come seeking that which belongs to me."

"What is that?"

He yanked on her, pulling her into the chamber. "The wealth of Draygon belongs to me!" he hissed. "No one else shall have it!"

Catrine ended up on her knees, the porridge half spilled. He slapped the bowl from her hand, finishing the job of spraying it all over the floor and onto Catrine's dress. Usually, he wore robes of the bishop who had come to Draygon to discover what had become of the king's nephew, and today was no exception. He wore those tattered robes as a monument to the chaotic kingdom he had created, a kingdom where he controlled his vassals as a player would control a pieces upon a game board. When he'd killed the bishop, he assumed those robes like a trophy.

Catrine had feared him greatly after that. She'd always been afraid of a man who was more animal than a man, someone they referred to as the Creature or the evil in the tower. So many names for one man, for one wicked wretch, and as she looked at him, she could feel herself succumbing to that fear she'd always felt for him. But the dynamic was different—with Hermes in the castle, with him providing such courage for her weary soul, the fear didn't cripple her as it usually did.

The embers of bravery began to burn.

"He is not here for the treasure," she said, picking up the bowl. "I've brought you food, but if you'd only rather shout at me and toss your food around, then I shall leave."

He grabbed her arm again, and the bowl went flying this time. "Like your mother, you are," he said in a threatening tone. "She was willful and disobedient."

"She was not."

He lifted his bushy eyebrows. "What's this?" he said. "You argue with me?"

"I am not arguing," Catrine said, trying not to surrender to her natural fear of him. "I was simply saying that she was not disobedient and the knight is not here for the treasure. He does not care about it."

The man stared at her for quite some time before his eyes narrowed as if a thought had just occurred to him. "And he shall never have the chance to reconsider," he said. "Tell Bennet I wish to see him."

Catrine knew what that meant. God help her, she knew. Whenever he summoned Bennet, it was to tell her brother to kill and strip the bones. There was virtually no other contact between them other than that, so she knew why he wanted to see Bennet.

He means to kill Hermes.

She simply couldn't allow it. All of the years of fear welled up inside her, tipping the scale in the direction of self-preservation and bravery. The spirit in her, the natural valor, had been suppressed for so long that she almost didn't recognize it. It took her a moment to realize what the sensation was, and she knew, as she lived and breathed, that she could not let anything happen to Hermes.

In a surprising show of strength, Catrine yanked her arm from his grip and backed away, out of arm's reach.

"Nay," she said, her voice trembling. "I'll not summon Bennet. You've no reason to kill the knight. He's not done anything wrong."

"Send him to me now."

"I will not."

He wasn't used to a refusal from her. At first, it puzzled him. Catrine could see the confusion ripping through his deep-set eyes. But very quickly, it enraged him.

"What did you say to me?"

"I said that I will not summon Bennet. I will not let you kill the knight."

The next thing Catrine realized, there was a club sailing at her head. She didn't even know where he got it, because she'd hardly seen him move to get it, but suddenly a big club with spikes on the end of it was flying right at her head.

With a scream, Catrine began to run.

The evil in the tower pursued.

CHAPTER FOURTEEN

I T WAS GISLA who heard the screaming first.

Carrying a wooden tray laden with bowls of porridge, sour wine, and the remainder of the bread that Catrine had made, she was heading in the direction of Bennet's chamber. She'd already taken the stairs and was preparing to turn to the left, to the corridor where the heavy, crumbling iron door that signified Bennet's sanctuary was located, when she heard the echo of screams coming from the tower.

Startled, she came to a halt, puzzled by the noise. It caught her off guard. But then she began hearing more screaming, and it sounded like someone was in a panic. Drawn by the sounds, she headed toward the tower and poked her head inside the door to see what the trouble was. Since the stairwell had an open center, she could see the scuffling high above, and it took her little time to see that Catrine was trying to run from a man in robes, who had her by the hair.

The screams were coming from Catrine.

Gisla dropped the tray, spraying porridge and wine all over the floor as she ran in the direction of Bennet's chamber. She bolted past the main staircase, into the corridor that led to Bennet's bower, all the while calling Bennet's name. In fact, she was shrieking it rather loudly, and those cries roused one of the other occupants of Draygon Castle.

Lord Marmion.

As Gisla went on the run for Bennet and Hermes, Lord Marmion's wardrobe opened, both doors, and he stepped out with his rusted weapon lodged firmly in his hand. He began fighting unseen foes again, but the screams were somehow penetrating his veil of madness. He could hear them when, in fact, he hadn't heard anything in the world of reality for years. He swung his sword around and killed at least two phantom soldiers before pausing, cocking his head when the screams grew louder. Sword in hand, he began to fight his way up the main staircase, following the sounds from the tower.

Meanwhile, Gisla was running so fast that she slammed into Bennet's door, pounding on it frantically.

"Bennet!" she cried. "Come quickly! Catrine is being attacked!"

She could hear voices, and within a few seconds, Hermes yanked the door open, his features taut with concern.

"Where is she?" he demanded. "What's happened?"

Gisla was out of breath, pointing in the direction she had come. "The stairwell to the tower," she said. "She is being attacked!"

Hermes took off at a run. Terrified, Gisla struggled to catch her breath when a big figure suddenly appeared in the doorway. She turned to see Bennet standing there, pulling a tunic over his head. That in and of itself wasn't shocking, but the fact that he wasn't covered with the cloak was. He hadn't concealed himself in the least. He had a pair of breeches on that he was trying to quickly secure, and the big, rumpled tunic draped over his large frame. His dark, curly hair was shaggy to his shoulders, and a full beard covered his face and part of his neck. It was the first time Gisla had seen him uncovered in over ten years, and she gasped at the sight.

"What is it?" Bennet turned to her, concerned. "What is happening?"

Gisla's eyes instantly filled with tears, spilling over before she could stop herself. "Oh…Bennet," she breathed.

He frowned. "What?" he demanded. "What is it?"

She smiled, shaking her head to let him know that it was nothing terrible. She flicked a tear away.

"'Tis only that I'd forgotten how handsome you are," she whispered. "It is so good to see you again."

Bennet stared at her, realizing as she did that he wasn't covered from head to toe. He'd dressed so quickly when she pounded on the door that there hadn't been time to find his cloak. As he realized that, his first reaction was to run back into the chamber and hide from her, but he fought the urge. Gisla wasn't running from him and wasn't ridiculing him. Not that she ever had, but he'd kept himself hidden from her to prevent the possibility. As it was, she was looking at him with great admiration.

He'd never forget the glow in her eyes.

At the moment, his fears and petty concerns didn't matter. His selfish sense of self-preservation didn't matter. Cloak or no cloak had no bearing. Nothing mattered except the fact that Catrine was in trouble, and he had to help her, no matter what he looked like.

"Where is my sister, love?" he asked, more gently.

Gisla wiped quickly at her eyes. "That way," she said, pointing toward the tower. "Hurry, Ben."

He did, but not before he grabbed his sword, which was leaning against the hearth. He blew past Gisla, running for the tower as she followed behind. Together, they entered the tower and began racing up the staircase, only to notice that Catrine's screaming had abruptly stopped. By the time they arrived, behind Hermes, they could see that the evil in the tower had Catrine by the hair and by the throat. With his arm across her neck as he pulled her against him, the implication was obvious.

He meant to kill her.

"Ah," he said in that thin, raspy voice. "I see that the cries of the disobedient wench have been heard throughout Draygon, for the Dragon and his cohorts have arrived. How noble."

Hermes was the closest. He was tense, prepared to pounce as he put a booted foot on the next step. "Let her go," he growled. "Release her and I may show mercy. Refuse and I will ensure you suffer the most painful death possible."

"Stop," the man said, tightening his grip. "Come closer and I shall snap her neck in front of you."

"If you do, you will regret that the rest of your miserable and short life."

"Mayhap," he said. "But the power, for the moment, is mine. You may punish me, but she will be dead. Is that what you want?"

That was true. There was logic in that short but serious statement. As Hermes pondered that, he looked the man over. The tower was illuminated by the daylight streaming in through the strategically placed lancet windows, and Hermes took a long look at the nephew of the king who had been controlling Draygon with lies for a decade.

He was an old man, with red hair that had gone mostly white, teeth that had turned green, and bony fingers that gripped Catrine painfully. He looked every inch the evil in the tower of legend, for there was nothing about him that seemed kind or redeemable. In his grip, Catrine had her eyes tightly shut as if she was warding off what was happening to her, and Hermes saw, at that moment, that she needed to be his one and only focus. His first instinct was to be nasty and threatening to the man who held her, but he suspected that wouldn't have the desired effect. Therefore, he'd have to do what did not come naturally to him.

He'd have to negotiate.

"So you have the power," he said after a moment. "Why do you hold her hostage? What do you want?"

The man's gaze moved to Bennet, standing behind Hermes because the stairs were narrow. "*You,*" he said. "You should have killed him when he first came to Draygon. Now he has returned and has done what you should not have allowed. He has come for that which does not belong to him."

Bennet didn't normally face the evil in the tower unless it had to do with death and destruction. In fact, he tried to pretend the man did not exist, but that was not always a simple thing. There was no denying that the evil *did* exist and had for years. But seeing that evil wrapped up around Catrine did something to Bennet—the years of ignoring the evil, of wallowing in self-pity and desolation, suddenly seemed like a waste of time. Catrine—dear Catrine—was in danger right before his very eyes, and it was not something he could tolerate any longer. The evil had always put her in danger, but it was something Bennet never saw for himself. He only heard of it afterward or perhaps discussed it beforehand, too consumed with his own problems to lend concern for his sister.

But this…this was right before his eyes.

His little sister on the brink of death.

"It does not belong to you, either," he rumbled. "It has never belonged to you. You came here, uninvited, to seduce my mother, and once you finally got her into your bed, you killed my father for trying to protect her. Nothing at Draygon belongs to you, and I am ashamed to say that it took a stranger pointing that out for me to realize it. Let my sister go and you may go in peace, but harm her and I will pull you limb from limb personally. I will not tell you again."

The man seemed confused by Bennet's statement, but only for a short moment. His thin face flushed red and his arm across Catrine's neck tightened. "It is *mine*," he said. "Your mother promised it to me. She promised to deliver it to me!"

"She never knew where it was. It is a secret only passed down from father to son."

The man's right hand went to Catrine's shoulder, and his dirty nails dug into her flesh as she yelped. "Then I was right to damn you with the curse," he snarled, spittle flying from his lips. "You are a despicable, filthy excuse for a man. You were bad enough as a boy, but as a man, you are a failure. An unworthy failure to the Draygon legacy."

"Let my sister go."

"Never!"

Bennet looked at Hermes, who caught his expression. Silent words passed between them, and they knew what they had to do. The time for talk had passed and the time for action had come, or Catrine might be in real trouble.

They began to mount the stairs in the man's direction.

The evil in the tower was brave when the tides were in his favor, but when they turned against him, he was as weak as a kitten. When he saw that Hermes and Bennet planned to take Catrine from him by force, and he knew that killing her would only hasten his agonizing demise, so he abruptly released her and shoved her away from him. Unfortunately, the stair railing was meager, and she slipped through it, screaming as she fell.

Hermes was closer. He managed to grab Catrine by the wrist as she tumbled past him and over the side, and suddenly, he found himself holding her as she dangled over a hard stone floor three stories below. It had happened so fast that he hadn't time to be terrified, but when he saw her hanging above a fall that would be fatal, fear took hold.

So did a sickening sense of déjà vu.

"Help me! Oh, God, help me!"

As Bennet rushed past him, after the man who was running for his tower room, Hermes was faced with his worst nightmare. *My dream!* The events of his recurring dream were returning full force, only this wasn't a dream. It was reality. Catrine wasn't dangling over a raging sea, but a rocky floor that would kill her just as quickly. Suddenly, Hermes was in the midst of that dream again, and he knew at that moment that it had been a warning. That dream, for years, had been a warning leading to this very moment.

Finally, he'd found the woman he was meant to save.

And save her he would.

"I have you," he said steadily, grabbing her wrist with both hands and pulling her toward him. "Hold tight, sweetheart. I have you. *I have you.*"

But Catrine was panicking. "I'm slipping!" she cried. "Hermes, I'm slipping!"

"Nay, you are not," he said, trying to brace himself so he could pull her up. He was a strong man, but he needed some leverage. "Stop twisting about. Just relax. I will pull you up, I swear."

"Hurry!"

"I am, I promise."

Catrine was weeping in fear. Hermes managed to pull her up enough that she could get a grip on the railing. Gisla was there, as she had been all along, and she rushed to grab Catrine's other hand. Between Hermes and Gisla, they managed to pull Catrine up and onto the flight of stairs. Hermes fell back against the wall, both arms around Catrine, never more terrified in his entire life nor more grateful that this situation had not ended like his dream had, time and time again.

The ending was different.

Catrine was alive.

As he held her tightly, he could hear sounds of a fight overhead as Bennet caught up to the man in the tower. He'd apparently grabbed the end of the man's robe and tripped him up, preventing him from continuing, and there was some kicking and fighting going on. Hermes didn't want to let Catrine go after having the scare of his life, but it sounded as if Bennet might need some help. With a heavy sigh, one of relief, he released Catrine long enough to get a good look at her. When he was satisfied that she was whole and unharmed, he kissed her on the forehead and prepared to let her go.

But then something strange happened.

A figure rushed past them up the stairs, a small figure with a weapon. Startled, both Hermes and Catrine watched as Lord Marmion ran up the steps, up to where Bennet was currently being kicked in the face. Shocked, Hermes stood up and craned his neck back in time to see Lord Marmion leap over Bennet, sword arcing, and slash the blade right into the chest of the Creature in the tower. For all of those phantom soldiers Lord Marmion fought on a daily basis, for all of the ghosts he grappled with over the years since that head injury in battle, he'd finally engaged a real man.

And he killed the Creature.

It was a shocking moment.

As the nephew of King Henry bled out on the steps, Lord Marmion turned to Bennet and sheathed his bloodied sword.

"And now," he said softly, "my battle is finally over."

As Bennet, Hermes, Catrine, and Gisla watched in astonishment, Sir Gerald de Allington, Lord Marmion, headed back down the stairs and disappeared from the tower. Into his wardrobe he retreated, never to emerge fighting again.

This was the moment he'd been waiting for all along.

"My God," Catrine finally breathed, looking at Hermes with wide eyes. "Is it truly over? Is all of it truly over?"

Hermes didn't know what to say. His gaze lingered on Catrine before he craned his neck back again, looking up to Bennet about ten feet over his head.

"Is he dead?" Hermes asked.

Bennet was looking at the still-twitching body. "If he is not, he soon will be," he said. Then he looked down at Hermes. "God's bones… It is *truly* over."

Struggling to overcome his shock, Hermes could only nod. Then he looked at Catrine. With pale and tear-stained cheeks, she met his gaze before smiling timidly.

"Thank you," she whispered. "For saving my life, for everything you have done for us. I will never be able to thank you enough, Hermes."

Hermes returned her smile. "Agreeing to be my wife is thanks enough," he murmured, cupping her face in his big hands. "It *is* over, Catrine. The curse, the control. Everything is over, I swear it. I will help you and Bennet rebuild. I will try to help you regain what you lost."

She smiled broadly, putting her hands over his. "That you should be so generous and kind to us is beyond my comprehension," she said. "But mayhap I am not supposed to comprehend it. Mayhap I am simply to have faith in it. I've never had much faith, you know."

"Nor have I," he said. "All I know is that I was supposed to be here, at this moment in time. All of my wandering, all of the searching, brought me to the place where my dreams meant me to be. I was supposed to find my purpose here, and now, I have. With you. If you will have me."

She reached up and wound her arms around his neck. "Of course I will have you," she said. "I will have no other."

Hermes kissed her sweetly on the lips before releasing her. "Bennet?" he said, rather loudly as he gazed into Catrine's eyes. "Your sister has consented to be my wife. What say you?"

Bennet was coming down the stairs now, his focus on Gisla as she stood against the wall near Hermes and Catrine. He was still red and scaly, blistered and rough, but he could see by the look in Gisla's eyes that she didn't care. She never had, and it had all been his own lack of courage that sent her away. The vinegar that Hermes had used on him was already doing some work; he could feel the redness and the pain easing just a little. It didn't feel as throbbing and sore as it usually did.

Better still, the sense of self-preservation he had when it came to Gisla wasn't there. It was gone, along with any reservations or doubts he'd ever had.

Perhaps Hermes had been right all along.

Perhaps it was time that Bennet reclaim his legacy.

"I say that you two deserve each other," he said after a moment, still looking at Gisla. "Mayhap…mayhap the hope you have is catching. Mayhap I deserve some of it, too."

He meant with Gisla. She beamed at him, unshed tears glimmering in her eyes, and Bennet knew that this day was the beginning of the rest of his life. A good life. The dark secrets of Draygon were many and not to be overcome in a day, but now he had the courage to face them and change what he could change.

He had the courage to live his life.

As Hermes began to help Catrine down the steps, Bennet went to Gisla. She was still smiling at him, still tearful. After a moment, he held out his hand to her. She didn't hesitate in taking it.

At that moment, Bennet knew that everything would be all right.

Curse or no curse, secrets or no secrets, Bennet de la Pare would live in the light again.

EPILOGUE

Four Days Later

"HIS NAME WAS Ewan ap Llewelyn," Hermes was saying. "He was the son of Joan, Lady of Wales, and Llewelyn the Great, but he was the youngest child with no inheritance. Evidently, he saw that in Draygon, and with that, now you know everything I know. The curse of Castle Draygon has ended."

He was speaking to his cousin, Stephen du Rennic, commander of Castle Canaan. Upon receiving Hermes's hastily written missive, Stephen had mounted a light brigade and traveled swiftly to Castle Draygon, which was less than a day's ride from Castle Canaan. As Hermes finished the positively wild story about Castle Draygon, Stephen shielded his eyes from the sun as he looked up at the horrific walls.

"God's blood," he muttered. "I've only heard terrible things about Draygon, and I remember my father telling me to avoid it at all costs, but what you just told me… That goes beyond what even my father must have known. Henry's nephew, you say?"

Hermes nodded, glancing back at the bony walls. "Aye," he said.

"Son of John's bastard daughter, so he's only distantly related to Henry."

"But related enough."

"Exactly."

Stephen shook his head at the madness of it all. "So what do you want from me now that I'm here?" he said. "Draygon is not exactly an ally, Hermes."

Hermes nodded. "I realize that," he said. "But that is going to change. I am going to introduce you to the Dragon of Draygon, Bennet de la Pare. The truth is that he's a good man who has been given a terrible lot in life. But he wants to change that. With the wicked influence gone, he wants to work to change his legacy."

"What did you have in mind?"

Hermes pointed to the enormous castle. "He is willing to let you garrison the castle until he can muster his own army," he said. "I'll be here to help him, but we need de Wolfe to garrison it. Put it under your protection. Once Draygon is up to full strength, she'll be a powerful and invaluable ally in this part of the valley."

Stephen wasn't convinced. "But how? Draygon may be big, and strategic, but it's not exactly a rich castle. It'll take money to bring this place back."

Hermes grinned. "That is where you would be wrong," he said. "Remember that treasure I told you about? Bennet took me to the secret hiding place last night. It's full of gold and treasure, Stephen. You've never seen anything like it. With that kind of money, he can buy himself a great mercenary army and pay for them quite handsomely. Please, Stephen. It is important to me."

"Why?"

"Because I'm marrying de la Pare's sister, so Draygon will be related to de Wolfe by marriage."

Stephen chuckled softly. "You could have told me that from the start and there would have never been any question in my mind as to why we must be allied with Draygon," he said, clapping Hermes on the shoulder. "I am happy for you, Hermes. Truly happy. May you be blessed."

Hermes smiled. "I already am," he said. "Draygon has given me a new life and a new purpose. And I will not waste it."

Stephen seemed satisfied with everything, clapping Hermes on the shoulder once more before dropping his hand and gesturing to the wall of bones. His smile faded.

"But those bones, man," he said, frowning. "What are we to do about them? I'm terrified simply looking at it."

Hermes chuckled. "Those will be removed and the bodies buried in consecrated ground," he said. "Bennet has already been to see the local priests about it, and they have agreed. It will take a good deal of work to free them from the walls and then repair the stone, but de la Pare is willing to do it. And I am willing to help. It is that new purpose I speak of."

It seemed noble enough and positive enough. But there was still something bothering Stephen that Hermes hadn't addressed yet.

"What of the villagers who hate Draygon so?" he asked. "What are you going to do about them?"

"Bennet has already arranged for a local farmer to deliver free food and drink to them as an offering of peace," Hermes said. "I have a feeling their hatred will not last long if Bennet proves himself generous, and most especially will not last long with de Wolfe troops manning the castle. De la Pare intends to repair the reputation of Draygon, the one that his father and that bastard in the tower all but ruined."

"And you're going to help him."

"For my future wife's sake, I am."

Stephen understood. He understood even more when he finally met Catrine de la Pare, a truly lovely woman with a winning smile.

He couldn't have been happier for his cousin.

As for Hermes and Catrine, they were married less than a month later at the door of the local church by priests who had helped bury the bones from Draygon's walls. They had their wedding night in Catrine's chamber at Draygon, a room formerly scant and bedraggled, but with the reinvention of Draygon and the release of the legendary treasure, it had become a warm and comfortable chamber.

A perfect chamber to start a family in.

Hermes didn't waste any time.

His first taste of his new wife had been something to remember, sensations and feelings he thought he'd long forgotten. He'd taken women to his bed since his first wife had passed, but they were simply acts. Simply needs. No emotion, no feelings involved. But with Catrine, everything he'd ever remembered about love and devotion came rushing back to him and then some.

It was a night to remember.

Hot flesh against hot flesh melded, searing and scorching as Hermes's lips latched on to Catrine. She was so soft and warm, and to feel her against him with such closeness was more than he could bear. He moved his mouth away from hers, down her neck, seeking a heated nipple. Beneath him, Catrine squirmed and gasped, but Hermes held her slender body fast, hardly allowing her any movement at all. He didn't want her to squirm away from him as he greedily suckled her breasts, using his body weight to keep her from moving too much as he stroked her thighs.

Her legs were so very supple, and he wedged his big body in between them. He could smell her feminine musk, and it was intoxicating, filling his nostrils until he could hardly control himself. As he lifted himself up to mount her, he put a hand on his manhood to gently direct himself into her.

"Relax, sweetheart," he murmured against her forehead. "You will enjoy this, I promise."

Catrine, who had so far been loving every new experience, grew anxious. His fingers, and his great shaft, were touching a place she'd rarely touched herself. It was very sensitive, and as he stroked her tenderly, her entire body quivered in a way she could not control.

"I…I *am* relaxed," she breathed, although it was a lie. "I know that this is how a husband touches a wife. This is how—"

He thrust forward, abruptly silencing her, filling her with his maleness as she gasped at the new sensation. A feeling of fullness she could never have anticipated, of closeness and intimacy that she had never imagined. Hermes was atop her, filling her body with his, and Catrine forgot all about her apprehension. Already, she loved the feeling of being impaled by a man. It was perhaps just the least bit painful at first, but her body was accommodating him quickly.

Already, she craved him.

Instinctively, her hands move to his buttocks, her nails gliding along his flesh, and Hermes groaned as he began to thrust. She was incredibly tight as he drove into her body with measured force, consumed by a world of warmth that revolved around the woman in his embrace. As he made love to his wife, one thought, and one alone, rolled through his head.

She is mine.

The woman from my dreams is mine.

It was joy beyond measure.

Nine months later, the result of that dream was born after a day and a night of a relatively easy labor. Catrine had hardly suffered at all, while Hermes had suffered horribly. Mabel's death in childbirth was all he could think about, knowing he could never survive another event like that, so when Gisla, now Lady de la Pare, assured him that his wife had delivered the child easily, Hermes didn't believe it until he saw it for himself. When his beautiful, lusty son was put into his arms,

Hermes realized that no dream he'd ever had could compare with the reality of what his life had become.

It had become heaven.

Little Ares de Norville joined his older siblings, Mabel's twins, in a very happy life at Castle Draygon. Most importantly, the wanderer that was once Hermes de Norville had found a home, and the hell once suffered by Catrine de la Pare had found salvation. But it wasn't simply Catrine; it was also Bennet and Gisla and even Hester, who now had a full and enriched life laid out before them. Whatever legends and curses had plagued Castle Draygon were no more, and whatever demons had plagued Hermes had been slain. Hermes had needed Draygon, and Draygon had needed Hermes.

Two torments, a prophetic dream, and one redemption.

When the legend of the Castle of Bones was told throughout the centuries, it was used as a cautionary tale to men who believed there was no hope and no redemption left in the world. For Hermes and Catrine, Bennet and Gisla, theirs was indeed a world filled with hope and love, and where the generosity of one man, in search of his own salvation, had ended up saving more than simply himself.

He'd saved his entire world.

And found the love of a lifetime.

✳ THE END ✳

AUTHOR'S AFTERWORD

So—the question is: what affliction did Bennet have that disfigured him so badly? The answer is simple—he had psoriasis that was compounded by severe cystic acne. Take those two in concert with each other and you have a horrific affliction that is painful and, in Medieval times, easily construed as a "curse." The Creature in the tower was a smart man—well versed in medicines—and he knew how to exacerbate it. Severe cystic acne is life-changing and, indeed, painful and horrible for those afflicted by it. Both of my children had it in early teenage years, but it can come on as late as someone's twenties.

The remedies that Hermes gave Bennet are indeed natural remedies that have been known to soothe and ease the redness of cystic acne as well as psoriasis. If you've read any of the de Wolfe Pack series, then you know that Hermes's grandfather, Paris de Norville, was a great healer in his own right, and Hermes clearly learned that skill. Nowadays, of course, there is prescription medicine to clear things up, but eight hundred years ago, they could only work with what they had on hand—and Hermes did.

Medieval medicine makes for interesting reading!

Kathryn Le Veque Novels

Medieval Romance:

De Wolfe Pack Series:
Warwolfe
The Wolfe
Nighthawk
ShadowWolfe
DarkWolfe
A Joyous de Wolfe Christmas
BlackWolfe
Serpent
A Wolfe Among Dragons
Scorpion
StormWolfe
Dark Destroyer
The Lion of the North
Walls of Babylon
The Best Is Yet To Be
BattleWolfe
Castle of Bones

De Wolfe Pack Generations:
WolfeHeart
WolfeStrike
WolfeSword
WolfeBlade
WolfeLord
WolfeShield
Nevermore

The Executioner Knights:
By the Unholy Hand
The Mountain Dark
Starless

A Time of End
Winter of Solace
Lord of the Sky
Splendid Hour
The Whispering Night
Netherworld
Lord of the Shadows
Of Mortal Fury

The de Russe Legacy:
The Falls of Erith
Lord of War: Black Angel
The Iron Knight
Beast
The Dark One: Dark Knight
The White Lord of Wellesbourne
Dark Moon
Dark Steel
A de Russe Christmas Miracle
Dark Warrior

The de Lohr Dynasty:
While Angels Slept
Rise of the Defender
Steelheart
Shadowmoor
Silversword
Spectre of the Sword
Unending Love
Archangel
A Blessed de Lohr Christmas

The Brothers de Lohr:
The Earl in Winter

Lords of East Anglia:
While Angels Slept
Godspeed
Age of Gods and Mortals

Great Lords of le Bec:
Great Protector

House of de Royans:
Lord of Winter
To the Lady Born
The Centurion

Lords of Eire:
Echoes of Ancient Dreams
Blacksword
The Darkland

Ancient Kings of Anglecynn:
The Whispering Night
Netherworld

Battle Lords of de Velt:
The Dark Lord
Devil's Dominion
Bay of Fear
The Dark Lord's First Christmas
The Dark Spawn
The Dark Conqueror
The Dark Angel

Reign of the House of de Winter:
Lespada
Swords and Shields

De Reyne Domination:
Guardian of Darkness
A Cold Wynter's Knight
With Dreams
The Fallen One
Black Storm

House of d'Vant:
Tender is the Knight (House of d'Vant)
The Red Fury (House of d'Vant)

The Dragonblade Series:
Fragments of Grace
Dragonblade
Island of Glass
The Savage Curtain
The Fallen One

Great Marcher Lords of de Lara
Dragonblade

House of St. Hever
Fragments of Grace
Island of Glass
Queen of Lost Stars

Lords of Pembury:
The Savage Curtain

**Lords of Thunder: The de Shera
Brotherhood Trilogy**
The Thunder Lord
The Thunder Warrior
The Thunder Knight

The Great Knights of de Moray:
Shield of Kronos
The Gorgon

The House of De Nerra:
The Promise
The Falls of Erith
Vestiges of Valor
Realm of Angels

Highland Warriors of Munro:
The Red Lion
Deep Into Darkness

The House of de Garr:

Lord of Light
Realm of Angels

Saxon Lords of Hage:
The Crusader
Kingdom Come

High Warriors of Rohan:
High Warrior

The House of Ashbourne:
Upon a Midnight Dream

The House of D'Aurilliac:
Valiant Chaos

The House of De Dere:
Of Love and Legend

St. John and de Gare Clans:
The Warrior Poet

The House of de Bretagne:
The Questing

The House of Summerlin:
The Legend

The Kingdom of Hendocia:
Kingdom by the Sea

Regency Historical Romance:
Sin Like Flynn: A Regency Historical
Romance Duet

Gothic Regency Romance:
Emma

Contemporary Romance:

Kathlyn Trent/Marcus Burton Series:
Valley of the Shadow
The Eden Factor
Canyon of the Sphinx

**The American Heroes Anthology
Series:**
The Lucius Robe
Fires of Autumn
Evenshade
Sea of Dreams
Purgatory

**Other non-connected Contemporary
Romance:**
Lady of Heaven
Darkling, I Listen
In the Dreaming Hour
River's End
The Fountain

Sons of Poseidon:
The Immortal Sea

**Pirates of Britannia Series (with Eliza
Knight):**
Savage of the Sea by Eliza Knight
Leader of Titans by Kathryn Le Veque
The Sea Devil by Eliza Knight
Sea Wolfe by Kathryn Le Veque

Note: All Kathryn's novels are designed to be read as stand-alones, although many have cross-over characters or cross-over family groups. Novels that are grouped together have related characters or family groups. You will notice that some series have the same books; that is because they are cross-overs. A hero in one book may be the secondary character in another.

There is NO reading order except by chronology, but even in that case, you can still read the books as stand-alones. No novel is connected to another by a cliff hanger, and every book has an HEA.

Series are clearly marked. All series contain the same characters or family groups except the American Heroes Series, which is an anthology with unrelated characters.

For more information, find it in **A Reader's Guide to the Medieval World of Le Veque**.

ABOUT KATHRYN LE VEQUE

Bringing the Medieval to Romance

KATHRYN LE VEQUE is a critically acclaimed, multiple USA TODAY Bestselling author, an Indie Reader bestseller, a charter Amazon All-Star author, and a #1 bestselling, award-winning, multi-published author in Medieval Historical Romance with over 100 published novels.

Kathryn is a multiple award nominee and winner, including the winner of Uncaged Book Reviews Magazine 2017 and 2018 "Raven Award" for Favorite Medieval Romance. Kathryn is also a multiple RONE nominee (InD'Tale Magazine), holding a record for the number of nominations. In 2018, her novel WARWOLFE was the winner in the Romance category of the Book Excellence Award and in 2019, her novel A WOLFE AMONG DRAGONS won the prestigious RONE award for best pre-16th century romance.

Kathryn is considered one of the top Indie authors in the world with over 2M copies in circulation, and her novels have been translated into several languages. Kathryn recently signed with Sourcebooks

Casablanca for a Medieval Fight Club series, first published in 2020.

In addition to her own published works, Kathryn is also the President/CEO of Dragonblade Publishing, a boutique publishing house specializing in Historical Romance. Dragonblade's success has seen it rise in the ranks to become Amazon's #1 e-book publisher of Historical Romance (K-Lytics report July 2020).

Kathryn loves to hear from her readers. Please find Kathryn on Facebook at Kathryn Le Veque, Author, or join her on Twitter @kathrynleveque. Sign up for Kathryn's blog at www.kathryn leveque.com for the latest news and sales.